A Smile of Fortune

A Smile of Fortune

A Harbour Story

Joseph Conrad

ET REMOTISSIMA PROPE

Modern Voices

Modern Voices
Published by Hesperus Press Limited
4 Rickett Street, London SW6 1RU
www.hesperuspress.com

First published in *London Magazine* in 1911
First published by Hesperus Press Limited, 2007

Foreword © Salley Vickers, 2007

Designed and typeset by Fraser Muggeridge studio
Printed in Jordan by the Jordan National Press

ISBN: 1-84391-428-X
ISBN13: 978-1-84391-428-0

Contents

Foreword

Conrad is best known for his sea stories, born out of his crucially formative years in the merchant navy. The sea is by no means the sole arena in Conrad's wise and impressive fiction, but it is true that the stories that are set at sea have about them an especially intimate tone, the authority that comes from well-digested personal experience.

The ironically titled *A Smile of Fortune* concerns a young ship's captain, who has made a passage to a Pacific island (which he dubs the 'Pearl') to pick up a cargo of sugar cane. As with so many of Conrad's principal male characters, the captain is at a period in his life where he feels that he is being tested: tested in his seamanship and his manhood alike. We are aware that he is a man of depth and philosophical temperament, the kind of man Conrad loves to write about: something of a loner, though clearly a man of sensibility and social polish, who looks at life with a wry and often wary eye:

> Why must the sea be used for trade – and for war as well? Why kill and traffic on it, pursuing selfish aims of no great importance after all? It would have been so much nicer just to sail about with here and there a port and a bit of land to stretch one's legs on, buy a few books and get a change of cooking for a while. But, living in a world more or less homicidal and desperately mercantile, it was plainly my duty to make the best of its opportunities.

Conrad is not generally considered a comic writer and yet in all his work there is a strain of dark humour arising from his acute observation of humankind's evasion of self-awareness and its ready capacity to get hold of the wrong end of the stick. Even the most intelligent of Conrad's characters – and for me one important source of enjoyment in his work is that while his characters are not intellectual they are very often highly intelligent – blunders, or has his most confident expectations confounded. In this case, the comedy revolves around the captain's mistaking of a ship-chandler called Jacobus – who wastes no time in handsomely, and lucratively, reprovisioning the ship when they anchor – for his brother, a merchant, whom the captain has been advised by his owners to consult over prospective business opportunities.

As so often in Conrad, the characters encountered are objective co-relatives for elements in the principal character's psyche. In this instance, the brothers Jacobus represent twin strains in the captain – the merchant brother he has been steered towards by the ship's owners reflecting the worldliness and outer social respectability that it is his professional duty to serve, the other brother embodying something at once more shady and alluring. For the ship-chandler brother turns out to be something of a social pariah. He has a secret, or not a secret exactly, more of an open scandal. He has been the victim of an infatuation with a circus 'artiste' whose daughter – who may or may not be his own – he has taken into his establishment and care. This erotic misadventure has earned him the disdainful distance of the local community, as opposed to the other, 'respected', brother, a 'bachelor all his life', whose natural 'mulatto' son our captain witnesses being brutally ill-treated by his father.

The sharp contrast between the behaviours of the two brothers provokes a crisis of consciousness in the captain. 'The grotesque image of a fat, pushing ship-chandler, enslaved by an unholy love-spell, fascinated me... What a strange victim for the gods!' It becomes clear that while one brother is condemned by society the other is looked up to, and yet the captain's own instinctive sympathy is all for the condemned. Almost as an act of social rebellion, but with the cover of needing some bags for his cargo that the ship-chandler might be able to supply, he accepts the oft-repeated invitation to visit the ship-chandler's home where he meets his 'daughter' Alice.

What follows is a mixture of acutely captured psychology, humour and pathos, as Conrad, with immense subtlety, conveys how an act of social defiance can precipitate the breakdown of other, inward, barriers. The captain, who becomes as fascinated by the daughter as his host was by the mother, finds further reasons to visit the house, and we witness him redoubling his efforts to engage her interest.

> How weak, irrational, and absurd we are! How easily carried away whenever our awakened imagination brings us the irritating hint of a desire! I cared for the girl in a particular way, seduced by the moody expression of her face, by her obstinate silences, her rare, scornful words; by the perpetual pout of her closed lips, the black depths of her fixed gaze turned slowly upon me as if in contemptuous provocation, only to be averted next moment with an exasperating indifference.

Alice is a Bertha Rochester figure, with an undertow in her makeup of restless simmering violence. We speculate that it is this that excites the captain, since it faces him with the enticing violence of his own, hitherto undisclosed, desire. 'Even her indifference was seductive. I felt myself growing attached to her by the bond of an irrealisable desire... It was like being the slave of some depraved habit.' The captain's passion once ignited, he is revealed to us as a very different man from the detached speculative figure of the opening pages. His pursuit of the girl is a series of thwarted sallies, until finally, enraged by her persistent rejections, he catches her in a savage embrace. The embrace is highly charged and explicitly erotic and the lone high-heeled shoe, which the girl leaves behind in her flight, is contemporary in its iconic appeal. And then, at the height of this eruption of emotion, something unaccountable occurs. Alice's father appears out of the shadows and it seems he may have witnessed the embrace. For a moment the world stands still for the captain and then, as swiftly, it reverses. Caught in the embarrassment of being observed, he agrees to the deal that the cajoling ship-chandler has been pressing on him, a consignment of potatoes for which he has neither room in the ship, sufficient funds, nor aptitude or inclination to trade. And yet, the audience of the father, which sabotages the erotic bond, is the precursor to this prosaic exchange. In a flash, desire mysteriously dies in the captain just as we observe it kindled in the recalcitrant girl.

The captain's desire cannot survive the scrutiny of a comprehending third presence, which lifts what has been fiercely secret into the cool, accounting gaze of the objective world. Conrad's insight is positively Freudian and the last pages of the story are a piece of darkly brilliant irony. Not only does the reluctant purchase of the potatoes prove a gold mine but the recognition of the betrayal of his own desire is too much for the captain's fragile equilibrium. On learning that his owners have heard from the merchant Jacobus, and wish their employee to return to the island to renew trade, the captain resigns his post, unequal to re-encountering the object of his fickle desire. Shaken by the picture of himself revealed by this brief – yet, we surmise, enduringly significant – encounter, the captain leaves for home as a forlorn passenger, 'heavy-hearted at that parting, seeing all my plans destroyed, my modest future endangered...'

– Salley Vickers, 2007

A Smile of Fortune

A Harbour Story

Ever since the sun rose I had been looking ahead. The ship glided gently in smooth water. After a sixty days' passage I was anxious to make my landfall, a fertile and beautiful island of the tropics. The more enthusiastic of its inhabitants delight in describing it as the 'Pearl of the Ocean'. Well, let us call it the 'Pearl'. It's a good name. A pearl distilling much sweetness upon the world.

This is only a way of telling you that first-rate sugar cane is grown there. All the population of the Pearl lives for it and by it. Sugar is their daily bread, as it were. And I was coming to them for a cargo of sugar in the hope of the crop having been good and of the freights being high.

Mr Burns, my chief mate, made out the land first, and very soon I became entranced by this blue, pinnacled apparition, almost transparent against the light of the sky, a mere emanation, the astral body of an island risen to greet me from afar. It is a rare phenomenon, such a sight of the Pearl at sixty miles off. And I wondered half seriously whether it was a good omen, whether what would meet me in that island would be as luckily exceptional as this beautiful, dreamlike vision so very few seamen have been privileged to behold.

But horrid thoughts of business interfered with my enjoyment of an accomplished passage. I was anxious for success and I wished, too, to do justice to the flattering latitude of my owners' instructions contained in one noble phrase: 'We leave it to you to do the best you can with the ship.'... All the world being thus given me for a stage, my abilities appeared to me no bigger than a pinhead.

Meantime the wind dropped, and Mr Burns began to make disagreeable remarks about my usual bad luck. I believe it was his devotion for me that made him critically outspoken on every occasion. All the same, I would not have put up with his humours if it had not been my lot at one time to nurse him through a desperate illness at sea. After snatching him out of the jaws of death, so to speak, it would have been absurd to throw away such an efficient officer. But sometimes I wished he would dismiss himself.

We were late in closing in with the land, and had to anchor outside the harbour till next day. An unpleasant and unrestful night followed. In this roadstead, strange to us both, Burns and I remained on deck almost all the time. Clouds swirled down the porphyry crags under which we lay. The rising wind made a great bullying noise amongst the naked spars, with interludes of sad moaning. I remarked that we had been in luck to fetch the anchorage before dark. It would have been a nasty, anxious night to hang off a harbour under canvas. But my chief mate was uncompromising in his attitude.

'Luck, you call it, sir! Ay – our usual luck. The sort of luck to thank God it's no worse!'

And so he fretted through the dark hours, while I drew on my fund of philosophy. Ah, but it was an exasperating, weary, endless night, to be lying at anchor close under that black coast! The agitated water made snarling sounds all round the ship. At times a wild gust of wind out of a gully high up on the cliffs struck on our rigging a harsh and plaintive note like the wail of a forsaken soul.

I

By half-past seven in the morning, the ship being then inside the harbour at last and moored within a long stone's throw from the quay, my stock of philosophy was nearly exhausted. I was dressing hurriedly in my cabin when the steward came tripping in with a morning suit over his arm.

Hungry, tired, and depressed, with my head engaged inside a white shirt irritatingly stuck together by too much starch, I desired him peevishly to 'heave round with that breakfast'. I wanted to get ashore as soon as possible.

'Yes, sir. Ready at eight, sir. There's a gentleman from the shore waiting to speak to you, sir.'

This statement was curiously slurred over. I dragged the shirt violently over my head and emerged staring.

'So early!' I cried. 'Who's he? What does he want?'

On coming in from sea one has to pick up the conditions of an utterly unrelated existence. Every little event at first has the peculiar emphasis of novelty. I was greatly surprised by that early caller; but there was no reason for my steward to look so particularly foolish.

'Didn't you ask for the name?' I enquired in a stern tone.

'His name's Jacobus, I believe,' he mumbled shamefacedly.

'Mr Jacobus!' I exclaimed loudly, more surprised than ever, but with a total change of feeling. 'Why couldn't you say so at once?'

But the fellow had scuttled out of my room. Through the momentarily opened door I had a glimpse of a tall, stout man standing in the cuddy by the table on which the cloth was already laid; a 'harbour' tablecloth, stainless and dazzlingly white. So far good.

I shouted courteously through the closed door that I was dressing and would be with him in a moment. In return the assurance that there was no hurry reached me in the visitor's deep, quiet undertone. His time was my own. He dared say I would give him a cup of coffee presently.

'I am afraid you will have a poor breakfast,' I cried apologetically. 'We have been sixty-one days at sea, you know.'

A quiet little laugh, with a 'That'll be all right, Captain,' was his answer. All this, words, intonation, the glimpsed attitude of the man in the cuddy, had an unexpected character, a something friendly in it – propitiatory. And my surprise was not diminished thereby. What did this call mean? Was it the sign of some dark design against my commercial innocence?

Ah! These commercial interests – spoiling the finest life under the sun. Why must the sea be used for trade – and for war as well? Why kill and traffic on it, pursuing selfish aims of no great importance after all? It would have been so much nicer just to sail about with here and there a port and a bit of land to stretch one's legs on, buy a few books and get a change of cooking for a while. But, living in a world more or less homicidal and desperately mercantile, it was plainly my duty to make the best of its opportunities.

My owners' letter had left it to me, as I have said before, to do my best for the ship, according to my own judgement. But it contained also a postscript worded somewhat as follows:

Without meaning to interfere with your liberty of action we are writing by the outgoing mail to some of our business friends there who may be of assistance to you. We desire you particularly to call on Mr Jacobus, a prominent merchant and charterer. Should you hit it off with him he may be able to put you in the way of profitable employment for the ship.

Hit it off! Here was the prominent creature absolutely on board asking for the favour of a cup of coffee! And life not being a fairy tale the improbability of the event almost shocked me. Had I discovered an enchanted nook of the earth where wealthy merchants rush fasting on board ships before they are fairly moored? Was this white magic or merely some black trick of trade? I came in the end (while making the bow of my tie) to suspect that perhaps I did not get the name right. I had been thinking of the prominent Mr Jacobus pretty frequently during the passage and my hearing might have been deceived by some remote similarity of sound... The steward might have said Antrobus – or maybe Jackson.

But coming out of my stateroom with an interrogative 'Mr Jacobus?' I was met by a quiet 'Yes,' uttered with a gentle smile. The 'yes' was rather perfunctory. He did not seem to make much of the fact that he was Mr Jacobus. I took stock of a big, pale face, hair thin on the top, whiskers also thin, of a faded non-descript colour, heavy eyelids. The thick, smooth lips in repose looked as if glued together. The smile was faint. A heavy, tranquil man. I named my two officers, who just then came down to breakfast, but why Mr Burns's silent demeanour should suggest suppressed indignation I could not understand.

While we were taking our seats round the table some disconnected words of an altercation going on in the companionway reached my ear. A stranger apparently wanted to come down to interview me, and the steward was opposing him.

'You can't see him.'

'Why can't I?'

'The Captain is at breakfast, I tell you. He'll be going on shore presently, and you can speak to him on deck.'

'That's not fair. You let – '

'I've had nothing to do with that.'

'Oh, yes, you have. Everybody ought to have the same chance. You let that fellow – '

The rest I lost. The person having been repulsed successfully, the steward came down. I can't say he looked flushed – he was a mulatto – but he looked flustered. After putting the dishes on the table he remained by the sideboard with that lackadaisical air of indifference he used to assume when he had done something too clever by half and was afraid of getting into a scrape over it. The contemptuous expression of Mr Burns's face as he looked from him to me was really extraordinary. I couldn't imagine what new bee had stung the mate now.

The Captain being silent, nobody else cared to speak, as is the way in ships. And I was saying nothing simply because I had been made dumb by the splendour of the entertainment. I had expected the usual sea breakfast, whereas I beheld spread before us a veritable feast of shore provisions: eggs, sausages, butter that plainly did not come from a Danish tin, cutlets, and even a dish of potatoes. It was three weeks since I had seen a real, live potato. I contemplated them with interest, and Mr Jacobus disclosed himself as a man of human, homely sympathies, and something of a thought-reader.

'Try them, Captain,' he encouraged me in a friendly undertone. 'They are excellent.'

'They look that,' I admitted. 'Grown on the island, I suppose.'

'Oh, no, imported. Those grown here would be more expensive.'

I was grieved at the ineptitude of the conversation. Were these the topics for a prominent and wealthy merchant to discuss? I thought the simplicity with which he made himself at home rather attractive, but what is one to talk about to a man who comes on one suddenly, after sixty-one days at sea, out of a totally unknown little town in an island one has never seen before? What were (besides sugar) the interests of that crumb of the earth, its gossip, its topics of conversation? To draw him on business at once would have been almost indecent – or even worse: impolitic. All I could do at the moment was to keep on in the old groove.

'Are the provisions generally dear here?' I asked, fretting inwardly at my inanity.

'I wouldn't say that,' he answered placidly, with that appearance of saving his breath his restrained manner of speaking suggested.

He would not be more explicit, yet he did not evade the subject. Eyeing the table in a spirit of complete abstemiousness (he wouldn't let me help him to any eatables) he went into details of supply. The beef was for the most part imported from

Madagascar; mutton of course was rare and somewhat expensive, but good goat's flesh –

'Are these goat's cutlets?' I exclaimed hastily, pointing at one of the dishes.

Posed sentimentally by the sideboard, the steward gave a start.

'Lor', no, sir! It's real mutton!'

Mr Burns got through his breakfast impatiently, as if exasperated by being made a party to some monstrous foolishness, muttered a curt excuse, and went on deck. Shortly afterwards the second mate took his smooth red countenance out of the cabin. With the appetite of a schoolboy, and after two months of sea fare, he appreciated the generous spread. But I did not. It smacked of extravagance. All the same, it was a remarkable feat to have produced it so quickly, and I congratulated the steward on his smartness in a somewhat ominous tone. He gave me a deprecatory smile and, in a way I didn't know what to make of, blinked his fine dark eyes in the direction of the guest.

The latter asked under his breath for another cup of coffee, and nibbled ascetically at a piece of very hard ship's biscuit. I don't think he consumed a square inch in the end, but meantime he gave me, casually as it were, a complete account of the sugar crop, of the local business houses, of the state of the freight market. All that talk was interspersed with hints as to personalities, amounting to veiled warnings, but his pale, fleshy face remained equable, without a gleam, as if ignorant of his voice. As you may imagine I opened my ears very wide. Every word was precious. My ideas as to the value of business friendship were being favourably modified. He gave me the names of all the disponible ships together with their tonnage and the names of their commanders. From that, which was still commercial information, he condescended to mere harbour gossip. The *Hilda* had unaccountably lost her figurehead in the Bay of Bengal, and her captain was greatly affected by this. He and the ship had been getting on in years together and the old gentleman imagined this strange event to be the forerunner of his own early dissolution. The *Stella* had experienced awful weather off the Cape – had her decks swept, and the chief officer washed overboard. And only a few hours before reaching port the baby died.

Poor Captain H— and his wife were terribly cut up. If they had only been able to bring it into port alive it could have been probably saved, but the wind failed them for the last week or so, light breezes, and... the baby was going to be buried this afternoon. He supposed I would attend –

'Do you think I ought to?' I asked, shrinkingly.

He thought so, decidedly. It would be greatly appreciated. All the captains in the harbour were going to attend. Poor Mrs H— was quite prostrated. Pretty hard on H— altogether.

'And you, Captain – you are not married I suppose?'

'No, I am not married,' I said. 'Neither married nor even engaged.'

Mentally I thanked my stars, and while he smiled in a musing, dreamy fashion, I expressed my acknowledgments for his visit and for the interesting business information he had been good enough to impart to me. But I said nothing of my wonder thereat.

'Of course, I would have made a point of calling on you in a day or two,' I concluded.

He raised his eyelids distinctly at me, and somehow managed to look rather more sleepy than before.

'In accordance with my owners' instructions,' I explained. 'You have had their letter, of course?'

By that time he had raised his eyebrows too but without any particular emotion. On the contrary he struck me then as absolutely imperturbable.

'Oh! You must be thinking of my brother.'

It was for me, then, to say 'Oh!' But I hope that no more than civil surprise appeared in my voice when I asked him to what, then, I owed the pleasure... He was reaching for an inside pocket leisurely.

'My brother's a very different person. But I am well known in this part of the world. You've probably heard – '

I took a card he extended to me. A thick business card, as I lived! Alfred Jacobus – the other was Ernest – dealer in every description of ship's stores! Provisions salt and fresh, oils, paints, rope, canvas, etc., etc. Ships in harbour victualled by contract on moderate terms –

'I've never heard of you,' I said brusquely.

His low-pitched assurance did not abandon him.

'You will be very well satisfied,' he breathed out quietly.

I was not placated. I had the sense of having been circumvented somehow. Yet I had deceived myself – if there was any deception. But the confounded cheek of inviting himself to breakfast was enough to deceive any one. And the thought struck me: Why! The fellow had provided all these eatables himself in the way of business. I said, 'You must have got up mighty early this morning.'

He admitted with simplicity that he was on the quay before six o'clock waiting for my ship to come in. He gave me the impression that it would be impossible to get rid of him now.

'If you think we are going to live on that scale,' I said, looking at the table with an irritated eye, 'you are jolly well mistaken.'

'You'll find it all right, Captain. I quite understand.'

Nothing could disturb his equanimity. I felt dissatisfied, but I could not very well fly out at him. He had told me many useful things – and besides he was the brother of that wealthy merchant. That seemed queer enough.

I rose and told him curtly that I must now go ashore. At once he offered the use of his boat for all the time of my stay in port.

'I only make a nominal charge,' he continued equably. 'My man remains all day at the landing steps. You have only to blow a whistle when you want the boat.'

And, standing aside at every doorway to let me go through first, he carried me off in his custody after all. As we crossed the quarterdeck two shabby individuals stepped forward and in mournful silence offered me business cards that I took from them without a word under his heavy eye. It was a useless and gloomy ceremony. They were the touts of the other ship-chandlers, and he, placid at my back, ignored their existence.

We parted on the quay, after he had expressed quietly the hope of seeing me often 'at the store'. He had a smoking room for captains there, with newspapers and a box of 'rather decent cigars'. I left him very unceremoniously.

My consignees received me with the usual business heartiness, but their account of the state of the freight market was by no means so favourable as the talk of the wrong Jacobus had led me to expect. Naturally I became inclined now to put my trust in his version, rather. As I closed the door of the private office behind me I thought to myself, 'H'm. A lot of lies. Commercial diplomacy. That's the sort of thing a man coming from sea has got to expect. They would try to charter the ship under the market rate.'

In the big, outer room, full of desks, the chief clerk, a tall, lean, shaved person in immaculate white clothes and with a shiny, closely cropped black head on which silvery gleams came and went, rose from his place and detained me affably. Anything they could do for me, they would be most happy. Was I likely to call again in the afternoon? What? Going to a funeral? Oh, yes, poor Captain H—.

He pulled a long, sympathetic face for a moment, then, dismissing from this workaday world the baby, which had got ill in a tempest and had died from too much calm at sea, he asked me with a dental, sharklike smile – if sharks had false teeth – whether I had yet made my little arrangements for the ship's stay in port.

'Yes, with Jacobus,' I answered carelessly. 'I understand he's the brother of Mr Ernest Jacobus to whom I have an introduction from my owners.'

I was not sorry to let him know I was not altogether helpless in the hands of his firm. He screwed his thin lips dubiously.

'Why,' I cried, 'isn't he the brother?'

'Oh, yes… They haven't spoken to each other for eighteen years,' he added impressively after a pause.

'Indeed! What's the quarrel about?'

'Oh, nothing! Nothing that one would care to mention,' he protested primly. 'He's got quite a large business. The best ship-chandler here, without a doubt. Business is all very well, but there is such a thing as personal character, too, isn't there? Good morning, Captain.'

He went away mincingly to his desk. He amused me. He resembled an old maid, a commercial old maid, shocked by some impropriety. Was it a commercial impropriety? Commercial impropriety is a serious matter, for it aims at one's pocket. Or was he only a purist in conduct who disapproved of Jacobus doing his own touting? It was certainly undignified. I wondered how the merchant brother liked it. But then different countries, different customs. In a community so isolated and so exclusively 'trading' social standards have their own scale.

2

I would have gladly dispensed with the mournful opportunity of becoming acquainted by sight with all my fellow captains at once. However I found my way to the cemetery. We made a considerable group of bareheaded men in sombre garments. I noticed that those of our company most approaching to the now obsolete sea dog type were the most moved – perhaps because they had less 'manner' than the new generation. The old sea dog, away from his natural element, was a simple and sentimental animal. I noticed one – he was facing me across the grave – who was dropping tears. They trickled down his weather-beaten face like drops of rain on an old rugged wall. I learned afterwards that he was looked upon as the terror of sailors, a hard man; that he had never had wife or chick of his own, and that, engaged from his tenderest years in deep-sea voyages, he knew women and children merely by sight.

Perhaps he was dropping those tears over his lost opportunities, from sheer envy of paternity and in strange jealousy of a sorrow that he could never know. Man, and even the seaman, is a capricious animal, the creature and the victim of lost opportunities. But he made me feel ashamed of my callousness. I had no tears.

I listened with horribly critical detachment to that service I had had to read myself, once or twice, over childlike men who had died at sea. The words of hope and defiance, the winged words so inspiring in the free immensity of water and sky, seemed to fall wearily into the little grave. What was the use of asking Death where her sting was, before that small, dark hole in the ground? And then my thoughts escaped me altogether – away into matters of life – and no very high matters at that – ships, freights, business. In the instability of his emotions man resembles deplorably a monkey. I was disgusted with my thoughts – and I thought: Shall I be able to get a charter soon? Time's money... Will that Jacobus really put good business in my way? I must go and see him in a day or two.

Don't imagine that I pursued these thoughts with any precision. They pursued me rather: vague, shadowy, restless, shamefaced. Theirs was a callous, abominable, almost revolting, pertinacity. And it was the presence of that pertinacious ship-chandler that had started them. He stood mournfully amongst our little band of men from the sea, and I was angry at his presence, which, suggesting his brother the merchant, had caused me to become outrageous to myself. For indeed I had preserved some decency of feeling. It was only the mind that –

It was over at last. The poor father – a man of forty with black, bushy side-whiskers and a pathetic gash on his freshly shaved chin – thanked us all, swallowing his tears. But for some reason, either because I lingered at the gate of the cemetery being somewhat hazy as to my way back, or because I was the youngest, or ascribing my moodiness caused by remorse to some more worthy and appropriate sentiment, or simply because I was even more of a stranger to him than the others – he singled me out. Keeping at my side, he renewed his thanks, which I listened to in a gloomy, conscience-stricken silence. Suddenly he slipped one hand under my arm and waved the other after a tall, stout figure walking away by itself down a street in a flutter of thin, grey garments: 'That's a good fellow – a real good fellow' – he swallowed down a belated sob – 'this Jacobus.'

And he told me in a low voice that Jacobus was the first man to board his ship on arrival, and, learning of their misfortune, had taken charge of everything, volunteered to attend to all routine business, carried off the ship's papers on shore, arranged for the funeral –

'A good fellow. I was knocked over. I had been looking at my wife for ten days. And helpless. Just you think of that! The dear little chap died the very day we made the land. How I managed to take the ship in God alone knows! I couldn't see anything; I couldn't speak; I couldn't... You've heard, perhaps, that we lost our mate overboard on the passage? There was no one to do it for me. And the poor woman nearly crazy down below there all alone with the... By the Lord! It isn't fair.'

We walked in silence together. I did not know how to part from him. On the quay he let go my arm and struck fiercely his fist into the palm of his other hand.

'By God, it isn't fair!' he cried again. 'Don't you ever marry unless you can chuck the sea first... It isn't fair.'

I had no intention to 'chuck the sea', and when he left me to go aboard his ship I felt convinced that I would never marry. While I was waiting at the steps for Jacobus' boatman, who had gone off somewhere, the captain of the *Hilda* joined me, a slender silk umbrella in his hand and the sharp points of his archaic, Gladstonian shirt-collar framing a small, clean-shaved, ruddy face. It was wonderfully fresh for his age, beautifully modelled and lit up by remarkably clear blue eyes. A lot of white hair, glossy like spun glass, curled upwards slightly under the brim of his valuable, ancient, panama hat with a broad black ribbon. In the aspect of that vivacious, neat, little old man there was something quaintly angelic and also boyish.

He accosted me, as though he had been in the habit of seeing me every day of his life from my earliest childhood, with a whimsical remark on the appearance of a stout Negro woman who was sitting upon a stool near the edge of the quay. Presently he observed amiably that I had a very pretty little barque.

I returned this civil speech by saying readily, 'Not so pretty as the *Hilda*.'

At once the corners of his clear-cut, sensitive mouth dropped dismally.

'Oh, dear! I can hardly bear to look at her now.'

Did I know, he asked anxiously, that he had lost the figure-head of his ship; a woman in a blue tunic edged with gold, the face perhaps not so very, very pretty, but her bare white arms beautifully shaped and extended as if she were swimming? Did I? Who would have expected such a thing… After twenty years too!

Nobody could have guessed from his tone that the woman was made of wood; his trembling voice, his agitated manner gave to his lamentations a ludicrously scandalous flavour… Disappeared at night – a clear fine night with just a slight swell – in the Gulf of Bengal. Went off without a splash; no one in the ship could tell why, how, at what hour – after twenty years last October… Did I ever hear!…

I assured him sympathetically that I had never heard – and he became very doleful. This meant no good he was sure. There was something in it that looked like a warning. But when I remarked that surely another figure of a woman could be procured I found myself being soundly rated for my levity. The old boy flushed pink under his clear tan as if I had proposed something improper. One could replace masts, I was told, or a lost rudder – any working part of a ship; but where was the use of sticking up a new figurehead? What satisfaction? How could one care for it? It was easy to see that I had never been shipmates with a figurehead for over twenty years.

'A new figurehead!' he scolded in unquenchable indignation. 'Why! I've been a widower now for eight-and-twenty years come next May and I would just as soon think of getting a new wife. You're as bad as that fellow Jacobus.'

I was highly amused.

'What has Jacobus done? Did he want you to marry again, Captain?' I enquired in a deferential tone. But he was launched now and only grinned fiercely.

'Procure – indeed! He's the sort of chap to procure you anything you like for a price. I hadn't been moored here for an hour when he got on board and at once offered to sell me a figurehead he happens to have in his yard somewhere. He got

Smith, my mate, to talk to me about it. "Mr Smith," says I, "don't you know me better than that? Am I the sort that would pick up with another man's cast-off figurehead?" And after all these years too! The way some of you young fellows talk – '

I affected great compunction, and as I stepped into the boat I said soberly, 'Then I see nothing for it but to fit in a neat fiddle-head – perhaps. You know, carved scrollwork, nicely gilt.'

He became very dejected after his outburst.

'Yes. Scrollwork. Maybe. Jacobus hinted at that too. He's never at a loss when there's any money to be extracted from a sailorman. He would make me pay through the nose for that carving. A gilt fiddlehead did you say – eh? I dare say it would do for you. You young fellows don't seem to have any feeling for what's proper.'

He made a convulsive gesture with his right arm.

'Never mind. Nothing can make much difference. I would just as soon let the old thing go about the world with a bare cutwater,' he cried sadly. Then as the boat got away from the steps he raised his voice on the edge of the quay with comical animosity: 'I would! If only to spite that figurehead-procuring bloodsucker. I am an old bird here and don't you forget it. Come and see me on board some day!'

I spent my first evening in port quietly in my ship's cuddy, and glad enough was I to think that the shore life that strikes one as so pettily complex, discordant, and so full of new faces on first coming from sea, could be kept off for a few hours longer. I was however fated to hear the Jacobus note once more before I slept.

Mr Burns had gone ashore after the evening meal to have, as he said, 'a look round'. As it was quite dark when he announced his intention I didn't ask him what it was he expected to see. Some time about midnight, while sitting with a book in the saloon, I heard cautious movements in the lobby and hailed him by name.

Burns came in, stick and hat in hand, incredibly vulgarised by his smart shore togs, with a jaunty air and an odious twinkle in his eye. Being asked to sit down he laid his hat and stick on the table and after we had talked of ship affairs for a little while, 'I've been hearing pretty tales on shore about that ship-chandler fellow who snatched the job from you so neatly, sir.'

I remonstrated with my late patient for his manner of expressing himself. But he only tossed his head disdainfully. A pretty dodge indeed: boarding a strange ship with breakfast in two baskets for all hands and calmly inviting himself to the captain's table! Never heard of anything so crafty and so impudent in his life.

I found myself defending Jacobus' unusual methods.

'He's the brother of one of the wealthiest merchants in the port.' The mate's eyes fairly snapped green sparks.

'His grand brother hasn't spoken to him for eighteen or twenty years,' he declared triumphantly. 'So there!'

'I know all about that,' I interrupted loftily.

'Do you sir? H'm!' His mind was still running on the ethics of commercial competition. 'I don't like to see your good nature taken advantage of. He's bribed that steward of ours with a five-rupee note to let him come down – or ten for that matter. He don't care. He will shove that and more into the bill presently.'

'Is that one of the tales you have heard ashore?' I asked.

He assured me that his own sense could tell him that much. No; what he had heard on shore was that no respectable person in the whole town would come near Jacobus. He lived in a large old-fashioned house in one of the quiet streets with a big garden. After telling me this Burns put on a mysterious air. 'He keeps a girl shut up there who, they say – '

'I suppose you've heard all this gossip in some eminently respectable place?' I snapped at him in a most sarcastic tone.

The shaft told, because Mr Burns, like many other disagreeable people, was very sensitive himself. He remained as if thunderstruck, with his mouth open for some further communication, but I did not give him the chance. 'And, anyhow, what the deuce do I care?' I added, retiring into my room.

And this was a natural thing to say. Yet somehow I was not indifferent. I admit it is absurd to be concerned with the morals of one's ship-chandler, if ever so well connected, but his personality had stamped itself upon my first day in harbour, in the way you know.

After this initial exploit Jacobus showed himself anything but intrusive. He was out in a boat early every morning going round the ships he served, and occasionally remaining on board one of them for breakfast with the captain.

As I discovered that this practice was generally accepted, I just nodded to him familiarly when one morning, on coming out of my room, I found him in the cabin. Glancing over the table I saw that his place was already laid. He stood awaiting my appearance, very bulky and placid, holding a beautiful bunch of flowers in his thick hand. He offered them to my notice with a faint, sleepy smile. From his own garden; had a very fine old garden; picked them himself that morning before going out to business; thought I would like... He turned away. 'Steward, can you oblige me with some water in a large jar, please.'

I assured him jocularly, as I took my place at the table, that he made me feel as if I were a pretty girl, and that he mustn't be surprised if I blushed. But he was busy arranging his floral tribute at the sideboard. 'Stand it before the Captain's plate, steward, please.' He made this request in his usual undertone.

The offering was so pointed that I could do no less than to raise it to my nose, and as he sat down noiselessly he breathed out the opinion that a few flowers improved notably the appearance of a ship's saloon. He wondered why I did not have a shelf fitted all round the skylight for flowers in pots to take with me to sea. He had a skilled workman able to fit up shelves in a day, and he could procure me two or three dozen good plants –

The tips of his thick, round fingers rested composedly on the edge of the table on each side of his cup of coffee. His face remained immovable. Mr Burns was smiling maliciously to himself. I declared that I hadn't the slightest intention of turning my skylight into a conservatory only to keep the cabin table in a perpetual mess of mould and dead vegetable matter.

'Rear most beautiful flowers,' he insisted with an upward glance. 'It's no trouble really.'

'Oh, yes, it is. Lots of trouble,' I contradicted. 'And in the end some fool leaves the skylight open in a fresh breeze, a flick of salt water gets at them and the whole lot is dead in a week.'

Mr Burns snorted a contemptuous approval. Jacobus gave up the subject passively. After a time he unglued his thick lips to ask me if I had seen his brother yet. I was very curt in my answer.

'No, not yet.'

'A very different person,' he remarked dreamily and got up. His movements were particularly noiseless. 'Well – thank you, Captain. If anything is not to your liking please mention it to your steward. I suppose you will be giving a dinner to the office clerks presently.'

'What for?' I cried with some warmth. 'If I were a steady trader to the port I could understand it. But a complete stranger!... I may not turn up again here for years. I don't see why!... Do you mean to say it is customary?'

'It will be expected from a man like you,' he breathed out placidly. 'Eight of the principal clerks, the manager, that's nine, you three gentlemen, that's twelve. It needn't be very expensive. If you tell your steward to give me a day's notice – '

'It will be expected of me! Why should it be expected of me? Is it because I look particularly soft – or what?

His immobility struck me as dignified suddenly, his imperturbable quality as dangerous. 'There's plenty of time to think about that,' I concluded weakly with a gesture that tried to wave him away. But before he departed he took time to mention regretfully that he had not yet had the pleasure of seeing me at his 'store' to sample those cigars. He had a parcel of 6,000 to dispose of, very cheap.

'I think it would be worth your while to secure some,' he added with a fat, melancholy smile and left the cabin.

Mr Burns struck his fist on the table excitedly.

'Did you ever see such impudence! He's made up his mind to get something out of you one way or another, sir.'

At once feeling inclined to defend Jacobus, I observed philosophically that all this was business, I supposed. But my absurd mate, muttering broken disjointed sentences, such as, 'I cannot bear!... Mark my words!...' and so on, flung out of the cabin. If I hadn't nursed him through that deadly fever I wouldn't have suffered such manners for a single day.

3

Jacobus having put me in mind of his wealthy brother I concluded I would pay that business call at once. I had by that time heard a little more of him. He was a member of the Council, where he made himself objectionable to the authorities. He exercised a considerable influence on public opinion. Lots of people owed him money. He was an importer on a great scale of all sorts of goods. For instance, the whole supply of bags for sugar was practically in his hands. This last fact I did not learn till afterwards. The general impression conveyed to me was that of a local personage. He was a bachelor and gave weekly card parties in his house out of town, which were attended by the best people in the colony.

The greater, then, was my surprise to discover his office in shabby surroundings, quite away from the business quarter, amongst a lot of hovels. Guided by a black board with white lettering, I climbed a narrow wooden staircase and entered a room with a bare floor of planks littered with bits of brown paper and wisps of packing straw. A great number of what looked like wine cases were piled up against one of the walls. A lanky, inky, light yellow, mulatto youth, miserably long-necked and generally recalling a sick chicken, got off a three-legged stool behind a cheap deal desk and faced me as if gone dumb with fright. I had some difficulty in persuading him to take in my name, though I could not get from him the nature of his objection. He did it at last with an almost agonised reluctance that ceased to be mysterious to me when I heard him being sworn at menacingly with savage, suppressed growls, then audibly cuffed and finally kicked out without any concealment whatever, because he came back flying head foremost through the door with a stifled shriek.

To say I was startled would not express it. I remained still, like a man lost in a dream. Clapping both his hands to that part of his frail anatomy that had received the shock, the poor wretch said to me simply, 'Will you go in, please.' His lamentable self-possession was wonderful, but it did not do away with the incredibility of the experience. A preposterous notion that I had seen this boy somewhere before, a thing obviously impossible, was like a delicate finishing touch of weirdness added to a scene fit to raise doubts as to one's sanity. I stared anxiously about me like an awakened somnambulist.

'I say,' I cried loudly, 'there isn't a mistake, is there? This is Mr Jacobus' office.'

The boy gazed at me with a pained expression – and somehow so familiar! A voice within growled offensively, 'Come in, come in, since you are there... I didn't know.'

I crossed the outer room as one approaches the den of some unknown wild beast: with intrepidity but in some excitement. Only no wild beast that ever lived would rouse one's indignation; the power to do that belongs to the odiousness of the human brute. And I was very indignant, which did not prevent me from being at once struck by the extraordinary resemblance of the two brothers.

This one was dark instead of being fair like the other, but he was as big. He was without his coat and waistcoat; he had been doubtless snoozing in the rocking chair that stood in a corner furthest from the window. Above the great bulk of his crumpled white shirt, buttoned with three diamond studs, his round face looked swarthy. It was moist; his brown moustache hung limp and ragged. He pushed a common, cane-bottomed chair towards me with his foot.

'Sit down.'

I glanced at it casually, then, turning my indignant eyes full upon him, I declared in precise and incisive tones that I had called in obedience to my owners' instructions.

'Oh! Yes. H'm! I didn't understand what that fool was saying... But never mind! It will teach the scoundrel to disturb me at this time of the day,' he added, grinning at me with savage cynicism.

I looked at my watch. It was past three o'clock – quite the full swing of afternoon office work in the port. He snarled imperiously: 'Sit down, Captain.'

I acknowledged the gracious invitation by saying deliberately, 'I can listen to all you may have to say without sitting down.'

Emitting a loud and vehement 'Pshaw!' he glared for a moment, very round-eyed and fierce. It was like a gigantic tomcat spitting at one suddenly. 'Look at him!… What do you fancy yourself to be? What did you come here for? If you won't sit down and talk business you had better go to the devil.'

'I don't know him personally,' I said. 'But after this I wouldn't mind calling on him. It would be refreshing to meet a gentleman.'

He followed me, growling behind my back, 'The impudence! I've a good mind to write to your owners what I think of you.'

I turned on him for a moment: 'As it happens I don't care. For my part I assure you I won't even take the trouble to mention you to them.'

He stopped at the door of his office while I traversed the littered anteroom. I think he was somewhat taken aback.

'I will break every bone in your body,' he roared suddenly at the miserable mulatto lad, 'if you ever dare to disturb me before half-past three for anybody. D'ye hear? For anybody!… Let alone any damned skipper,' he added, in a lower growl.

The frail youngster, swaying like a reed, made a low moaning sound. I stopped short and addressed this sufferer with advice. It was prompted by the sight of a hammer (used for opening the wine cases, I suppose) that was lying on the floor.

'If I were you, my boy, I would have that thing up my sleeve when I went in next and at the first occasion I would – '

What was there so familiar in that lad's yellow face? Entrenched and quaking behind the flimsy desk, he never looked up. His heavy, lowered eyelids gave me suddenly the clue of the puzzle. He resembled – yes, those thick glued lips – he resembled the brothers Jacobus. He resembled both, the wealthy merchant and the pushing shopkeeper (who resembled each other); he resembled them as much as a thin, light-yellow mulatto lad may resemble a big, stout, middle-aged white man. It was the exotic complexion and the slightness of his build that had put me off so completely. Now I saw in him unmistakably the Jacobus strain, weakened, attenuated, diluted as it were in a bucket of water – and I refrained from finishing my speech. I had intended to say: 'Crack this brute's head for him.' I still felt the conclusion to be sound. But it is no trifling responsibility to counsel parricide to any one, however deeply injured.

'Beggarly – cheeky – skippers.'

I despised the emphatic growl at my back; only, being much vexed and upset, I regret to say that I slammed the door behind me in a most undignified manner.

It may not appear altogether absurd if I say that I brought out from that interview a kindlier view of the other Jacobus. It was with a feeling resembling partisanship that, a few days later, I called at his 'store'. That long, cavern-like place of business, very dim at the back and stuffed full of all sorts of goods, was entered from the street by a lofty archway. At the far end I saw my Jacobus exerting himself in his shirtsleeves among his assistants. The captains' room was a small, vaulted apartment with a stone floor and heavy iron bars in its windows like a dungeon converted to hospitable purposes. A couple of cheerful bottles and several gleaming glasses made a brilliant cluster round a tall, cool red earthenware pitcher on the centre table, which was littered with newspapers from all parts of the world. A well-groomed stranger in a smart grey check suit, sitting with one leg flung over his knee, put down one of these sheets briskly and nodded to me.

I guessed him to be a steamer-captain. It was impossible to get to know these men. They came and went too quickly and their ships lay moored far out, at the very entrance of the harbour. Theirs was another life altogether. He yawned slightly.

'Dull hole, isn't it?'

I understood this to allude to the town.

'Do you find it so?' I murmured.

'Don't you? But I'm off tomorrow, thank goodness.'

He was a very gentlemanly person, good-natured and superior. I watched him draw the open box of cigars to his side of the table, take a big cigar-case out of his pocket and begin to fill it very methodically. Presently, on our eyes meeting, he winked like a common mortal and invited me to follow his example. 'They are really decent smokes.' I shook my head.

'I am not off tomorrow.'

'What of that? Think I am abusing old Jacobus' hospitality? Heavens! It goes into the bill, of course. He spreads such little matters all over his account. He can take care of himself! Why, it's business – '

I noted a shadow fall over his well-satisfied expression, a momentary hesitation in closing his cigar-case. But he ended by putting it in his pocket jauntily. A placid voice uttered in the doorway: 'That's quite correct, Captain.'

The large noiseless Jacobus advanced into the room. His quietness, in the circumstances, amounted to cordiality. He had put on his jacket before joining us, and he sat down in the chair vacated by the steamer-man, who nodded again to me and went out with a short, jarring laugh. A profound silence reigned. With his drowsy stare Jacobus seemed to be slumbering open-eyed. Yet, somehow, I was aware of being profoundly scrutinised by those heavy eyes. In the enormous cavern of the store somebody began to nail down a case, expertly: tap-tap... tap-tap-tap.

Two other experts, one slow and nasal, the other shrill and snappy, started checking an invoice.

'A half-coil of three-inch manilla rope.'

'Right!'

'Six assorted shackles.'

'Right!'

'Six tins assorted soups, three of pâté, two asparagus, fourteen pounds tobacco, cabin.'

'Right!'

'It's for the captain who was here just now,' breathed out the immovable Jacobus. 'These steamer orders are very small. They pick up what they want as they go along. That man will be in Samarang in less than a fortnight. Very small orders indeed.'

The calling over of the items went on in the shop; an extraordinary jumble of varied articles, paintbrushes, Yorkshire Relish, etc., etc.... 'Three sacks of best potatoes,' read out the nasal voice.

At this Jacobus blinked like a sleeping man roused by a shake, and displayed some animation. At his order, shouted into the shop, a smirking half-caste clerk with his ringlets much oiled and with a pen stuck behind his ear, brought in a sample of six potatoes that he paraded in a row on the table.

Being urged to look at their beauty I gave them a cold and hostile glance. Calmly, Jacobus proposed that I should order ten or fifteen tons – tons! I couldn't believe my ears. My crew could not have eaten such a lot in a year, and potatoes (excuse these practical remarks) are a highly perishable commodity. I thought he was joking – or else trying to find out whether I was an unutterable idiot. But his purpose was not so simple. I discovered that he meant me to buy them on my own account.

'I am proposing you a bit of business, Captain. I wouldn't charge you a great price.'

I told him that I did not go in for trade. I even added grimly that I knew only too well how that sort of spec generally ended.

He sighed and clasped his hands on his stomach with exemplary resignation. I admired the placidity of his impudence. Then waking up somewhat, 'Won't you try a cigar, Captain?'

'No, thanks. I don't smoke cigars.'

'For once!' he exclaimed, in a patient whisper. A melancholy silence ensued. You know how sometimes a person discloses a certain unsuspected depth and acuteness of thought; that is, in other words, utters something unexpected. It was unexpected enough to hear Jacobus say, 'The man who just went out was right enough. You might take one, Captain. Here everything is bound to be in the way of business.'

I felt a little ashamed of myself. The remembrance of his horrid brother made him appear quite a decent sort of fellow. It was with some compunction that I said a few words to the effect that I could have no possible objection to his hospitality.

Before I was a minute older I saw where this admission was leading me. As if changing the subject, Jacobus mentioned that his private house was about ten minutes' walk away. It had a beautiful old walled garden. Something really remarkable. I ought to come round some day and have a look at it.

He seemed to be a lover of gardens. I too take extreme delight in them, but I did not mean my compunction to carry me as far as Jacobus' flower-beds, however beautiful and old. He added, with a certain homeliness of tone, 'There's only my girl there.'

It is difficult to set everything down in due order, so I must revert here to what happened a week or two before. The medical officer of the port had come on board my ship to have a look at one of my crew who was ailing, and naturally enough he was asked to step into the cabin. A fellow shipmaster of mine was there too, and in the conversation, somehow or other, the name of Jacobus came to be mentioned. It was pronounced with no particular reverence by the other man, I believe. I don't remember now what I was going to say. The doctor – a pleasant, cultivated fellow, with an assured manner – prevented me by striking in, in a sour tone, 'Ah! You're talking about my respected papa-in-law.'

Of course, that sally silenced us at the time. But I remembered the episode, and at this juncture, pushed for something noncommittal to say, I enquired with polite surprise, 'You have your married daughter living with you, Mr Jacobus?'

He moved his big hand from right to left quietly. No! That was another of his girls, he stated, ponderously and under his breath as usual. She… He seemed in a pause to be ransacking his mind for some kind of descriptive phrase. But my hopes were disappointed. He merely produced his stereotyped definition.

'She's a very different sort of person.'

'Indeed… And by the by, Jacobus, I called on your brother the other day. It's no great compliment if I say that I found him a very different sort of person from you.'

He had an air of profound reflection, then remarked quaintly, 'He's a man of regular habits.'

He might have been alluding to the habit of late siesta, but I mumbled something about 'beastly habits anyhow' – and left the store abruptly.

4

My little passage with Jacobus the merchant became known generally. One or two of my acquaintances made distant allusions to it. Perhaps the mulatto boy had talked. I must confess that people appeared rather scandalised, but not with Jacobus' brutality. A man I knew remonstrated with me for my hastiness.

I gave him the whole story of my visit, not forgetting the telltale resemblance of the wretched mulatto boy to his tormentor. He was not surprised. No doubt, no doubt. What of that? In a jovial tone he assured me that there must be many of that sort. The elder Jacobus had been a bachelor all his life. A highly respectable bachelor. But there had never been open scandal in that connection. His life had been quite regular. It could cause no offence to any one.

I said that I had been offended considerably. My interlocutor opened very wide eyes. Why? Because a mulatto lad got a few knocks? That was not a great affair, surely. I had no idea how insolent and untruthful these half-castes were. In fact he seemed to think Mr Jacobus rather kind than otherwise to employ that youth at all: a sort of amiable weakness that could be forgiven.

This acquaintance of mine belonged to one of the old French families, descendants of the old colonists: all noble, all impoverished, and living a narrow domestic life in dull, dignified decay. The men, as a rule, occupy inferior posts in Government offices or in business houses. The girls are almost always pretty, ignorant of the world, kind and agreeable and generally bilingual; they prattle innocently both in French and English. The emptiness of their existence passes belief.

I obtained my entry into a couple of such households because some years before, in Bombay, I had occasion to be of use to a pleasant, ineffectual young man who was rather stranded there, not knowing what to do with himself or even how to get home to his island again. It was a matter of 200 rupees or so, but, when I turned up, the family made a point of showing their gratitude by admitting me to their intimacy. My knowledge of the French language made me specially acceptable. They had meantime managed to marry the fellow to a woman nearly twice his age, comparatively well off: the only profession he was really fit for. But it was not all cakes and ale. The first time I called on the couple she spied a little spot of grease on the poor devil's pantaloons and made him a screaming scene of reproaches so full of sincere passion that I sat terrified as at a tragedy of Racine.

Of course there was never question of the money I had advanced him, but his sisters, Miss Angele and Miss Mary, and the aunts of both families, who spoke quaint archaic French of pre-Revolution period, and a host of distant relations adopted me for a friend outright in a manner that was almost embarrassing.

It was with the eldest brother (he was employed at a desk in my consignee's office) that I was having this talk about the merchant Jacobus. He regretted my attitude and nodded his head sagely. An influential man. One never knew when one would need him. I expressed my immense preference for the shopkeeper of the two. At that my friend looked grave.

'What on earth are you pulling that long face about?' I cried impatiently. 'He asked me to see his garden and I have a good mind to go some day.'

'Don't do that,' he said, so earnestly that I burst into a fit of laughter, but he looked at me without a smile.

This was another matter altogether. At one time the public conscience of the island had been mightily troubled by my Jacobus. The two brothers had been partners for years in great harmony, when a wandering circus came to the island and my Jacobus became suddenly infatuated with one of the lady riders. What made it worse was that he was married. He had not even the grace to conceal his passion. It must have been strong indeed to carry away such a large placid creature. His behaviour was perfectly scandalous. He followed that woman to the Cape, and apparently travelled at the tail of that beastly circus to other parts of the world, in a most degrading position. The woman soon ceased to care for him, and treated him worse than a dog. Most extraordinary stories of moral degradation were reaching the island at that time. He had not the strength of mind to shake himself free…

The grotesque image of a fat, pushing ship-chandler, enslaved by an unholy love-spell, fascinated me, and I listened rather open-mouthed to the tale as old as the world, a tale that had been the subject of legend, of moral fables, of poems, but that so ludicrously failed to fit the personality. What a strange victim for the gods!

Meantime his deserted wife had died. His daughter was taken care of by his brother, who married her as advantageously as was possible in the circumstances.

'Oh! The Mrs Doctor!' I exclaimed.

'You know that? Yes. A very able man. He wanted a lift in the world, and there was a good bit of money from her mother, besides the expectations… Of course, they don't know him,' he added. 'The doctor nods in the street, I believe, but he avoids speaking to him when they meet on board a ship, as must happen sometimes.'

I remarked that this surely was an old story by now.

My friend assented. But it was Jacobus' own fault that it was neither forgiven nor forgotten. He came back ultimately. But how? Not in a spirit of contrition, in a way to propitiate his scandalised fellow citizens. He must needs drag along with him a child – a girl…

'He spoke to me of a daughter who lives with him,' I observed, very much interested.

'She's certainly the daughter of the circus-woman,' said my friend. 'She may be his daughter too; I am willing to admit that she is. In fact I have no doubt – '

But he did not see why she should have been brought into a respectable community to perpetuate the memory of the scandal. And that was not the worst. Presently something much more distressing happened. That abandoned woman turned up. Landed from a mail boat…

'What! Here? To claim the child perhaps,' I suggested.

'Not she!' My friendly informant was very scornful. 'Imagine a painted, haggard, agitated, desperate hag. Been cast off in Mozambique by somebody who paid her passage here. She had been injured internally by a kick from a horse; she hadn't a cent on her when she got ashore; I don't think she even asked to see the child. At any rate, not till the last day of her life. Jacobus hired for her a bungalow to die in. He got a couple of Sisters from the hospital to nurse her through these few months. If he didn't marry her in extremis as the good Sisters tried to bring about, it's because she wouldn't even hear of it. As the nuns said: 'The woman died impenitent'. It was reported that she ordered Jacobus out of the room with her last breath. This may be the real reason why he didn't go into mourning himself; he only put the child into black. While she was little she was to be seen sometimes about the streets attended by a Negro woman, but since she became of age to put her hair up I don't think she has set foot outside that garden once. She must be over eighteen now.'

Thus my friend, with some added details, such as, that he didn't think the girl had spoken to three people of any position in the island; that an elderly female relative of the brothers Jacobus had been induced by extreme poverty to accept the position of gouvernante to the girl. As to Jacobus' business (which certainly annoyed his brother) it was a wise choice on his part. It brought him in contact only with strangers of passage, whereas any other would have given rise to all sorts of awkwardness with his social equals. The man was not wanting in a certain tact – only he was naturally shameless. For why did he want to keep that girl with him? It was most painful for everybody.

I thought suddenly (and with profound disgust) of the other Jacobus, and I could not refrain from saying slyly, 'I suppose if he employed her, say, as a scullion in his household and occasionally pulled her hair or boxed her ears, the position would have been more regular – less shocking to the respectable class to which he belongs.'

He was not so stupid as to miss my intention, and shrugged his shoulders impatiently.

'You don't understand. To begin with, she's not a mulatto. And a scandal is a scandal. People should be given a chance to forget. I dare say it would have been better for her if she had been turned into a scullion or something of that kind. Of course he's trying to make money in every sort of petty way, but in such a business there'll never be enough for anybody to come forward.'

When my friend left me I had a conception of Jacobus and his daughter existing, a lonely pair of castaways, on a desert island; the girl sheltering in the house as if it were a cavern in a cliff, and Jacobus going out to pick up a living for both on the beach – exactly like two shipwrecked people who always hope for some rescuer to bring them back at last into touch with the rest of mankind.

But Jacobus' bodily reality did not fit in with this romantic view. When he turned up on board in the usual course, he sipped the cup of coffee placidly, asked me if I was satisfied – and I hardly listened to the harbour gossip he dropped slowly in his low, voice-saving enunciation. I had then troubles of my own. My ship chartered, my thoughts dwelling on the success of a quick round voyage, I had been suddenly confronted by a shortage of bags. A catastrophe! The stock of one especial kind, called pockets, seemed to be totally exhausted. A consignment was shortly expected – it was afloat, on its way, but, meantime, the loading of my ship dead stopped, I had enough to worry about. My consignees, who had received me with such heartiness on my arrival, now, in the character of my charterers, listened to my complaints with polite helplessness. Their manager, the old-maidish, thin man, who so prudishly didn't even like to speak about the impure Jacobus, gave me the correct commercial view of the position.

'My dear Captain,' – he was retracting his leathery cheeks into a condescending, sharklike smile – 'we were not morally obliged to tell you of a possible shortage before you signed the charter party. It was for you to guard against the contingency of a delay – strictly speaking. But of course we shouldn't have taken any advantage. This is no one's fault really. We ourselves have been taken unawares,' he concluded primly, with an obvious lie.

This lecture I confess had made me thirsty. Suppressed rage generally produces that effect, and as I strolled on aimlessly I bethought myself of the tall earthenware pitcher in the captains' room of the Jacobus 'store'.

With no more than a nod to the men I found assembled there, I poured down a deep, cool draught on my indignation, then another, and then, becoming dejected, I sat plunged in cheerless reflections. The others read, talked, smoked, bandied over my head some unsubtle chaff. But my abstraction was respected. And it was without a word to any one that I rose and went out, only to be quite unexpectedly accosted in the bustle of the store by Jacobus the outcast.

'Glad to see you, Captain. What? Going away? You haven't been looking so well these last few days, I notice. Run down, eh?'

He was in his shirtsleeves, and his words were in the usual course of business, but they had a human note. It was commercial amenity, but I had been a stranger to amenity in that connection. I do verily believe (from the direction of his heavy glance towards a certain shelf) that he was going to suggest the purchase of Clarkson's Nerve Tonic, which he kept in stock, when I said impulsively, 'I am rather in trouble with my loading.'

Wide awake under his sleepy, broad mask with glued lips, he understood at once, had a movement of the head so appreciative that I relieved my exasperation by exclaiming, 'Surely there must be eleven hundred quarter-bags to be found in the colony. It's only a matter of looking for them.'

Again that slight movement of the big head, and in the noise and activity of the store that tranquil murmur, 'To be sure. But then people likely to have a reserve of quarter-bags wouldn't want to sell. They'd need that size themselves.'

'That's exactly what my consignees are telling me. Impossible to buy. Bosh! They don't want to. It suits them to have the ship hung up. But if I were to discover the lot they would have to – Look here, Jacobus! You are the man to have such a thing up your sleeve.'

He protested with a ponderous swing of his big head. I stood before him helplessly, being looked at by those heavy eyes with a veiled expression as of a man after some soul-shaking crisis. Then, suddenly, 'It's impossible to talk quietly here,' he whispered. 'I am very busy. But if you could go and wait for me in my house. It's less than ten minutes' walk. Oh, yes, you don't know the way.'

He called for his coat and offered to take me there himself. He would have to return to the store at once for an hour or so to finish his business, and then he would be at liberty to talk over with me that matter of quarter-bags. This programme was breathed out at me through slightly parted, still lips; his heavy, motionless glance rested upon me, placid as ever, the glance of a tired man – but I felt that it was searching, too. I could not imagine what he was looking for in me and kept silent, wondering.

'I am asking you to wait for me in my house till I am at liberty to talk this matter over. You will?'

'Why, of course!' I cried.

'But I cannot promise – '

'I dare say not,' I said. 'I don't expect a promise.'

'I mean I can't even promise to try the move I've in my mind. One must see first… h'm!'

'All right. I'll take the chance. I'll wait for you as long as you like. What else have I to do in this infernal hole of a port!'

Before I had uttered my last words we had set off at a swinging pace. We turned a couple of corners and entered a street completely empty of traffic, of semi-rural aspect, paved with cobblestones nestling in grass tufts. The house came to the line of the roadway, a single story on an elevated basement of rough stones, so that our heads were below the level of the windows as we went along. All the jalousies were tightly shut, like eyes, and the house seemed fast asleep in the afternoon sunshine. The entrance was at the side, in an alley even more grass-grown than the street: a small door, simply on the latch.

With a word of apology as to showing me the way, Jacobus preceded me up a dark passage and led me across the naked parquet floor of what I supposed to be the dining room. It was lighted by three glass doors that stood wide open on to a verandah or rather loggia running its brick arches along the garden side of the house. It was really a magnificent garden: smooth green lawns and a gorgeous maze of flower-beds in the foreground, displayed around a basin of dark water framed in a marble rim, and in the distance the massed foliage of varied trees concealing the roofs of other houses. The town might have been miles away. It was a brilliantly coloured solitude, drowsing in a warm, voluptuous silence. Where the long, still shadows fell across the beds, and in shady nooks, the massed colours of the flowers had an extraordinary magnificence of effect. I stood entranced. Jacobus grasped me delicately above the elbow, impelling me to a half-turn to the left.

I had not noticed the girl before. She occupied a low, deep, wickerwork armchair, and I saw her in exact profile like a figure in a tapestry, and as motionless. Jacobus released my arm.

'This is Alice,' he announced tranquilly, and his subdued manner of speaking made it sound so much like a confidential communication that I fancied myself nodding understandingly and whispering, 'I see, I see'. ... Of course, I did nothing of the kind. Neither of us did anything; we stood side by side looking down at the girl. For quite a time she did not stir, staring straight before her as if watching the vision of some pageant passing through the garden in the deep, rich glow of light and the splendour of flowers.

Then, coming to the end of her reverie, she looked round and up. If I had not at first noticed her, I am certain that she too had been unaware of my presence till she actually perceived me by her father's side. The quickened upward movement of the heavy eyelids, the widening of the languid glance, passing into a fixed stare, put that beyond doubt.

Under her amazement there was a hint of fear, and then came a flash as of anger. Jacobus, after uttering my name fairly loud, said, 'Make yourself at home, Captain – I won't be gone long,' and went away rapidly. Before I had time to make a bow I was left alone with the girl – who, I remembered suddenly, had not been seen by any man or woman of that town since she had found it necessary to put up her hair. It looked as though it had not been touched again since that distant time of first putting up; it was a mass of black, lustrous locks, twisted anyhow high on her head, with long, untidy wisps hanging down on each side of the clear sallow face; a mass so thick and strong and abundant that, nothing but to look at, it gave you a sensation of heavy pressure on the top of your head and an impression of magnificently cynical untidiness. She leaned forward, hugging herself with crossed legs; a dingy, amber-coloured, flounced wrapper of some thin stuff revealed the young supple body drawn together tensely in the deep low seat as if crouching for a spring. I detected a slight, quivering start or two, which looked uncommonly like bounding away. They were followed by the most absolute immobility.

The absurd impulse to run out after Jacobus (for I had been startled, too) once repressed, I took a chair, placed it not very far from her, sat down deliberately, and began to talk about the garden, caring not what I said, but using a gentle caressing intonation as one talks to soothe a startled wild animal. I could not even be certain that she understood me. She never raised her face nor attempted to look my way. I kept on talking only to prevent her from taking flight. She had another of those quivering, repressed starts that made me catch my breath with apprehension.

Ultimately I formed a notion that what prevented her perhaps from going off in one great, nervous leap was the scantiness of her attire. The wicker armchair was the most substantial thing about her person. What she had on under that dingy, loose, amber wrapper must have been of the most flimsy and airy character. One could not help being aware of it. It was obvious. I felt it actually embarrassing at first, but that sort of embarrassment is got over easily by a mind not enslaved by narrow prejudices. I did not avert my gaze from Alice. I went on talking with ingratiating softness, the recollection that, most likely, she had never before been spoken to by a strange man adding to my assurance. I don't know why an emotional tenseness should have crept into the situation. But it did. And just as I was becoming aware of it a slight scream cut short my flow of urbane speech.

The scream did not proceed from the girl. It was emitted behind me, and caused me to turn my head sharply. I understood at once that the apparition in the doorway was the elderly relation of Jacobus, the companion, the gouvernante. While she remained thunderstruck, I got up and made her a low bow.

The ladies of Jacobus' household evidently spent their days in light attire. This stumpy old woman with a face like a large wrinkled lemon, beady eyes, and a shock of iron-grey hair, was dressed in a garment of some ash-coloured, silky, light stuff. It fell from her thick neck down to her toes with the simplicity of an unadorned nightgown. It made her appear truly cylindrical. She exclaimed, 'How did you get here?'

Before I could say a word she vanished and presently I heard a confusion of shrill protestations in a distant part of the house.

Obviously no one could tell her how I got there. In a moment, with great outcries from two Negro women following her, she waddled back to the doorway, infuriated.

'What do you want here?'

I turned to the girl. She was sitting straight up now, her hands posed on the arms of the chair. I appealed to her.

'Surely, Miss Alice, you will not let them drive me out into the street?'

Her magnificent black eyes, narrowed, long in shape, swept over me with an indefinable expression, then in a harsh, contemptuous voice she let fall in French a sort of explanation, 'C'est papa.'

I made another low bow to the old woman.

She turned her back on me in order to drive away her black henchwomen, then surveying my person in a peculiar manner with one small eye nearly closed and her face all drawn up on that side as if with a twinge of toothache, she stepped out on the verandah, sat down in a rocking chair some distance away, and took up her knitting from a little table. Before she started at it she plunged one of the needles into the mop of her grey hair and stirred it vigorously.

Her elementary nightgown-sort of frock clung to her ancient, stumpy, and floating form. She wore white cotton stockings and flat brown velvet slippers. Her feet and ankles were obtrusively visible on the footrest. She began to rock herself slightly, while she knitted. I had resumed my seat and kept quiet, for I mistrusted that old woman. What if she ordered me to depart? She seemed capable of any outrage. She had snorted once or twice; she was knitting violently. Suddenly she piped at the young girl in French a question that I translate colloquially: 'What's your father up to, now?'

The young creature shrugged her shoulders so comprehensively that her whole body swayed within the loose wrapper, and in that unexpectedly harsh voice that yet had a seductive quality to the senses, like certain kinds of natural rough wines one drinks with pleasure: 'It's some captain. Leave me alone – will you!'

The chair rocked quicker, the old, thin voice was like a whistle. 'You and your father make a pair. He would stick at nothing – that's well known. But I didn't expect this.'

I thought it high time to air some of my own French. I remarked modestly, but firmly, that this was business. I had some matters to talk over with Mr Jacobus.

At once she piped out a derisive 'Poor innocent!' Then, with a change of tone, 'The shop's for business. Why don't you go to the shop to talk with him?'

The furious speed of her fingers and knitting needles made one dizzy, and with squeaky indignation: 'Sitting here staring at that girl – is that what you call business?'

'No,' I said suavely. 'I call this pleasure – an unexpected pleasure. And unless Miss Alice objects – '

I half turned to her. She flung at me an angry and contemptuous 'Don't care!' and leaning her elbow on her knees took her chin in her hand – a Jacobus chin undoubtedly. And those heavy eyelids, this black irritated stare reminded me of Jacobus, too – the wealthy merchant, the respected one. The design of her eyebrows also was the same, rigid and ill-omened. Yes! I traced in her a resemblance to both of them. It came to me as a sort of surprising remote inference that both these Jacobuses were rather handsome men after all. I said, 'Oh! Then I shall stare at you till you smile.'

She favoured me again with an even more viciously scornful 'Don't care!'

The old woman broke in blunt and shrill, 'Hear his impudence! And you too! Don't care! Go at least and put some more clothes on. Sitting there like this before this sailor riff-raff.'

The sun was about to leave the Pearl of the Ocean for other seas, for other lands. The walled garden full of shadows blazed with colour as if the flowers were giving up the light absorbed during the day. The amazing old woman became very explicit. She suggested to the girl a corset and a petticoat with a cynical unreserve that humiliated me. Was I of no more account than a wooden dummy? The girl snapped out: 'Shan't!'

It was not the naughty retort of a vulgar child; it had a note of desperation. Clearly my intrusion had somehow upset the balance of their established relations. The old woman knitted with furious accuracy, her eyes fastened down on her work.

'Oh, you are the true child of your father! And THAT talks of entering a convent! Letting herself be stared at by a fellow.'

'Leave off.'

'Shameless thing!'

'Old sorceress,' the girl uttered distinctly, preserving her meditative pose, chin in hand, and a faraway stare over the garden.

It was like the quarrel of the kettle and the pot. The old woman flew out of the chair, banged down her work, and with a great play of thick limb perfectly visible in that weird, clinging garment of hers, strode at the girl – who never stirred. I was experiencing a sort of trepidation when, as if awed by that unconscious attitude, the aged relative of Jacobus turned short upon me.

She was, I perceived, armed with a knitting needle, and as she raised her hand her intention seemed to be to throw it at me like a dart. But she only used it to scratch her head with, examining me the while at close range, one eye nearly shut and her face distorted by a whimsical, one-sided grimace.

'My dear man,' she asked abruptly, 'do you expect any good to come of this?'

'I do hope so indeed, Miss Jacobus.' I tried to speak in the easy tone of an afternoon caller. 'You see, I am here after some bags.'

'Bags! Look at that now! Didn't I hear you holding forth to that graceless wretch?'

'You would like to see me in my grave,' uttered the motionless girl hoarsely.

'Grave! What about me? Buried alive before I am dead for the sake of a thing blessed with such a pretty father!' she cried, and turning to me: 'You're one of these men he does business with. Well – why don't you leave us in peace, my good fellow?'

It was said in a tone – this 'leave us in peace!' There was a sort of ruffianly familiarity, a superiority, a scorn in it. I was to hear it more than once, for you would show an imperfect knowledge of human nature if you thought that this was my last visit to that house – where no respectable person had put foot for ever so many years. No, you would be very much mistaken if you imagined that this reception had scared me away. First of all I was not going to run before a grotesque and ruffianly old woman.

And then you mustn't forget these necessary bags. That first evening Jacobus made me stay to dinner; after, however, telling me loyally that he didn't know whether he could do anything at all for me. He had been thinking it over. It was too difficult, he feared… But he did not give it up in so many words.

We were only three at table; the girl by means of repeated 'Won't!' 'Shan't!' and 'Don't care!' having conveyed and affirmed her intention not to come to the table, not to have any dinner, not to move from the verandah. The old relative hopped about in her flat slippers and piped indignantly; Jacobus towered over her and murmured placidly in his throat; I joined jocularly from a distance, throwing in a few words, for which under the cover of the night I received secretly a most vicious poke in the ribs from the old woman's elbow or perhaps her fist. I restrained a cry. And all the time the girl didn't even condescend to raise her head to look at any of us. All this may sound childish – and yet that stony, petulant sullenness had an obscurely tragic flavour.

And so we sat down to the food around the light of a good many candles while she remained crouching out there, staring in the dark as if feeding her bad temper on the heavily scented air of the admirable garden.

Before leaving I said to Jacobus that I would come next day to hear if the bag affair had made any progress. He shook his head slightly at that.

'I'll haunt your house daily till you pull it off. You'll be always finding me here.'

His faint, melancholy smile did not part his thick lips.

'That will be all right, Captain.'

Then seeing me to the door, very tranquil, he murmured earnestly the recommendation, 'Make yourself at home,' and also the hospitable hint about there being always 'a plate of soup'. It was only on my way to the quay, down the ill-lighted streets, that I remembered I had been engaged to dine that very evening with the S— family. Though vexed with my forgetfulness (it would be rather awkward to explain) I couldn't help thinking that it had procured me a more amusing evening. And besides – business. The sacred business – .

In a barefooted Negro who overtook me at a run and bolted down the landing steps I recognised Jacobus' boatman, who must have been feeding in the kitchen. His usual 'Goodnight, sah!' as I went up my ship's ladder had a more cordial sound than on previous occasions.

5

I kept my word to Jacobus. I haunted his home. He was perpetually finding me there of an afternoon when he popped in for a moment from the 'store'. The sound of my voice talking to his Alice greeted him on his doorstep, and when he returned for good in the evening, ten to one he would hear it still going on in the verandah. I just nodded to him; he would sit down heavily and gently, and watch with a sort of approving anxiety my efforts to make his daughter smile.

I called her often 'Alice', right before him; sometimes I would address her as Miss 'Don't Care', and I exhausted myself in nonsensical chatter without succeeding once in taking her out of her peevish and tragic self. There were moments when I felt I must break out and start swearing at her till all was blue. And I fancied that had I done so Jacobus would not have moved a muscle. A sort of shady, intimate understanding seemed to have been established between us.

I must say the girl treated her father exactly in the same way she treated me.

And how could it have been otherwise? She treated me as she treated her father. She had never seen a visitor. She did not know how men behaved. I belonged to the low lot with whom her father did business at the port. I was of no account. So was her father. The only decent people in the world were the people of the island, who would have nothing to do with him because of something wicked he had done. This was apparently the explanation Miss Jacobus had given her of the household's isolated position. For she had to be told something! And I feel convinced that this version had been assented to by Jacobus. I must say the old woman was putting it forward with considerable gusto. It was on her lips the universal explanation, the universal allusion, the universal taunt.

One day Jacobus came in early and, beckoning me into the dining room, wiped his brow with a weary gesture and told me that he had managed to unearth a supply of quarter-bags.

'It's fourteen hundred your ship wanted, did you say, Captain?'

'Yes, yes!' I replied eagerly, but he remained calm. He looked more tired than I had ever seen him before.

'Well, Captain, you may go and tell your people that they can get that lot from my brother.'

As I remained open-mouthed at this, he added his usual placid formula of assurance, 'You'll find it correct, Captain.'

'You spoke to your brother about it?' I was distinctly awed. 'And for me? Because he must have known that my ship's the only one hung up for bags. How on earth – '

He wiped his brow again. I noticed that he was dressed with unusual care, in clothes in which I had never seen him before. He avoided my eye.

'You've heard people talk, of course… That's true enough. He… I… We certainly… for several years…' His voice declined to a mere sleepy murmur. 'You see I had something to tell him of, something that – '

His murmur stopped. He was not going to tell me what this something was. And I didn't care. Anxious to carry the news to my charterers, I ran back on the verandah to get my hat.

At the bustle I made the girl turned her eyes slowly in my direction, and even the old woman was checked in her knitting. I stopped a moment to exclaim excitedly, 'Your father's a brick, Miss Don't Care. That's what he is.'

She beheld my elation in scornful surprise. Jacobus with unwonted familiarity seized my arm as I flew through the dining room, and breathed heavily at me a proposal about 'A plate of soup' that evening. I answered distractedly, 'Eh? What? Oh, thanks! Certainly. With pleasure,' and tore myself away. Dine with him? Of course. The merest gratitude.

But some three hours afterwards, in the dusky, silent street, paved with cobblestones, I became aware that it was not mere gratitude that was guiding my steps towards the house with the old garden, where for years no guest other than myself had ever dined. Mere gratitude does not gnaw at one's interior economy in that particular way. Hunger might, but I was not feeling particularly hungry for Jacobus' food.

On that occasion, too, the girl refused to come to the table.

My exasperation grew. The old woman cast malicious glances at me. I said suddenly to Jacobus, 'Here! Put some chicken and salad on that plate.' He obeyed without raising his eyes. I carried it with a knife and fork and a serviette out on the verandah. The garden was one mass of gloom, like a cemetery of flowers buried in the darkness, and she, in the chair, seemed to muse mournfully over the extinction of light and colour. Only whiffs of heavy scent passed like wandering, fragrant souls of that departed multitude of blossoms. I talked volubly, jocularly, persuasively, tenderly; I talked in a subdued tone. To a listener it would have sounded like the murmur of a pleading lover. Whenever I paused expectantly there was only a deep silence. It was like offering food to a seated statue.

'I haven't been able to swallow a single morsel thinking of you out here starving yourself in the dark. It's positively cruel to be so obstinate. Think of my sufferings.'

'Don't care.'

I felt as if I could have done her some violence – shaken her, beaten her maybe. I said, 'Your absurd behaviour will prevent me coming here any more.'

'What's that to me?'

'You like it.'

'It's false,' she snarled.

My hand fell on her shoulder, and if she had flinched I verily believe I would have shaken her. But there was no movement and this immobility disarmed my anger.

'You do. Or you wouldn't be found on the verandah every day. Why are you here, then? There are plenty of rooms in the house. You have your own room to stay in – if you did not want to see me. But you do. You know you do.'

I felt a slight shudder under my hand and released my grip as if frightened by that sign of animation in her body. The scented air of the garden came to us in a warm wave like a voluptuous and perfumed sigh.

'Go back to them,' she whispered, almost pitifully.

As I re-entered the dining room I saw Jacobus cast down his eyes. I banged the plate on the table. At this demonstration of ill humour he murmured something in an apologetic tone, and I turned on him viciously as if he were accountable to me for these 'abominable eccentricities', I believe I called them.

'But I dare say Miss Jacobus here is responsible for most of this offensive manner,' I added loftily.

She piped out at once in her brazen, ruffianly manner, 'Eh? Why don't you leave us in peace, my good fellow?'

I was astonished that she should dare before Jacobus. Yet what could he have done to repress her? He needed her too much. He raised a heavy, drowsy glance for an instant, then looked down again. She insisted with shrill finality, 'Haven't you done your business, you two? Well, then – '

She had the true Jacobus impudence, that old woman. Her mop of iron-grey hair was parted, on the side like a man's, raffishly, and she made as if to plunge her fork into it, as she used to do with the knitting needle, but refrained. Her little black eyes sparkled venomously. I turned to my host at the head of the table – menacingly as it were.

'Well, and what do you say to that, Jacobus? Am I to take it that we have done with each other?'

I had to wait a little. The answer when it came was rather unexpected, and in quite another spirit than the question.

'I certainly think we might do some business yet with those potatoes of mine, Captain. You will find that – '

I cut him short.

'I've told you before that I don't trade.'

His broad chest heaved without a sound in a noiseless sigh.

'Think it over, Captain,' he murmured, tenacious and tranquil, and I burst into a jarring laugh, remembering how he had stuck to the circus-rider woman – the depth of passion under that placid surface, which even cuts with a riding whip (so the legend had it) could never raffle into the semblance of a storm; something like the passion of a fish would be if one could imagine such a thing as a passionate fish.

That evening I experienced more distinctly than ever the sense of moral discomfort that always attended me in that house lying under the ban of all 'decent' people. I refused to stay on and smoke after dinner, and when I put my hand into the thickly cushioned palm of Jacobus, I said to myself that it would be for the last time under his roof. I pressed his bulky paw heartily nevertheless. Hadn't he got me out of a serious difficulty? To the few words of acknowledgement I was bound, and indeed quite willing, to utter, he answered by stretching his closed lips in his melancholy, glued-together smile.

'That will be all right, I hope, Captain,' he breathed out weightily.

'What do you mean?' I asked, alarmed. 'That your brother might yet – '

'Oh, no,' he reassured me. 'He... he's a man of his word, Captain.'

My self-communion as I walked away from his door, trying to believe that this was for the last time, was not satisfactory. I was aware myself that I was not sincere in my reflections as to Jacobus' motives, and, of course, the very next day I went back again.

How weak, irrational, and absurd we are! How easily carried away whenever our awakened imagination brings us the irritating hint of a desire! I cared for the girl in a particular way, seduced by the moody expression of her face, by her obstinate silences, her rare, scornful words; by the perpetual pout of her closed lips, the black depths of her fixed gaze turned slowly upon me as if in contemptuous provocation, only to be averted next moment with an exasperating indifference.

Of course the news of my assiduity had spread all over the little town. I noticed a change in the manner of my acquaintances and even something different in the nods of the other captains, when meeting them at the landing steps or in the offices where business called me. The old-maidish head clerk treated me with distant punctiliousness and, as it were, gathered his skirts round him for fear of contamination. It seemed to me that the very niggers on the quays turned to look after me as I passed, and as to Jacobus' boatman, his 'Goodnight, sah!' when he put me on board was no longer merely cordial – it had a familiar, confidential sound as though we had been partners in some villainy.

My friend S— the elder passed me on the other side of the street with a wave of the hand and an ironic smile. The younger brother, the one they had married to an elderly shrew, he, on the strength of an older friendship and as if paying a debt of gratitude, took the liberty to utter a word of warning.

'You're doing yourself no good by your choice of friends, my dear chap,' he said with infantile gravity.

As I knew that the meeting of the brothers Jacobus was the subject of excited comment in the whole of the sugary Pearl of the Ocean I wanted to know why I was blamed.

'I have been the occasion of a move that may end in a reconciliation surely desirable from the point of view of the proprieties – don't you know?'

'Of course, if that girl were disposed of it would certainly facilitate – ' he mused sagely, then, inconsequential creature, gave me a light tap on the lower part of my waistcoat. 'You old sinner,' he cried jovially, 'much you care for proprieties. But you had better look out for yourself, you know, with a personage like Jacobus who has no sort of reputation to lose.'

He had recovered his gravity of a respectable citizen by that time and added regretfully, 'All the women of our family are perfectly scandalised.'

But by that time I had given up visiting the S— family and the D— family. The elder ladies pulled such faces when I showed myself, and the multitude of related young ladies received me with such a variety of looks: wondering, awed, mocking (except Miss Mary, who spoke to me and looked at me with hushed, pained compassion as though I had been ill), that I had no difficulty in giving them all up. I would have given up the society of the whole town, for the sake of sitting near that girl, snarling and superb and barely clad in that flimsy, dingy, amber wrapper, open low at the throat. She looked, with the wild wisps of hair hanging down her tense face, as though she had just jumped out of bed in the panic of a fire.

She sat leaning on her elbow, looking at nothing. Why did she stay listening to my absurd chatter? And not only that, but why did she powder her face in preparation for my arrival? It seemed to be her idea of making a toilette, and in her untidy negligence a sign of great effort towards personal adornment.

But I might have been mistaken. The powdering might have been her daily practice and her presence in the verandah a sign of an indifference so complete as to take no account of my existence. Well, it was all one to me.

I loved to watch her slow changes of pose, to look at her long immobilities composed in the graceful lines of her body, to observe the mysterious narrow stare of her splendid black eyes, somewhat long in shape, half closed, contemplating the void. She was like a spellbound creature with the forehead of a goddess crowned by the dishevelled magnificent hair of a gipsy tramp. Even her indifference was seductive. I felt myself growing attached to her by the bond of an irrealisable desire, for I kept my head – quite. And I put up with the moral discomfort of Jacobus' sleepy watchfulness, tranquil, and yet so expressive; as if there had been a tacit pact between us two. I put up with the insolence of the old woman's, 'Aren't you ever going to leave us in peace, my good fellow?' with her taunts; with her brazen and sinister scolding. She was of the true Jacobus stock, and no mistake.

Directly I got away from the girl I called myself many hard names. What folly was this? I would ask myself. It was like being the slave of some depraved habit. And I returned to her with my head clear, my heart certainly free, not even moved by pity for that castaway (she was as much of a castaway as any one ever wrecked on a desert island), but as if beguiled by some extraordinary promise. Nothing more unworthy could be imagined. The recollection of that tremulous whisper when I gripped her shoulder with one hand and held a plate of chicken with the other was enough to make me break all my good resolutions.

Her insulting taciturnity was enough sometimes to make one gnash one's teeth with rage. When she opened her mouth it was only to be abominably rude in harsh tones to the associate of her reprobate father, and the full approval of her aged relative was conveyed to her by offensive chuckles. If not that, then her remarks, always uttered in the tone of scathing contempt, were of the most appalling inanity.

How could it have been otherwise? That plump, ruffianly Jacobus old maid in the tight grey frock had never taught her any manners. Manners I suppose are not necessary for born castaways. No educational establishment could ever be induced to accept her as a pupil – on account of the proprieties, I imagine. And Jacobus had not been able to send her away anywhere. How could he have done it? Who with? Where to? He himself was not enough of an adventurer to think of settling down anywhere else. His passion had tossed him at the tail of a circus up and down strange coasts, but, the storm over, he had drifted back shamelessly where, social outcast as he was, he remained still a Jacobus – one of the oldest families on the island, older than the French even. There must have been a Jacobus in at the death of the last dodo... The girl had learned nothing, she had never listened to a general conversation, she knew nothing, she had heard of nothing. She could read certainly, but all the reading matter that ever came in her way were the newspapers provided for the captains' room of the 'store'. Jacobus had the habit of taking these sheets home now and then in a very stained and ragged condition.

As her mind could not grasp the meaning of any matters treated there except police-court reports and accounts of crimes, she had formed for herself a notion of the civilised world as a scene of murders, abductions, burglaries, stabbing affrays, and every sort of desperate violence. England and France, Paris and London (the only two towns of which she seemed to have heard), appeared to her sinks of abomination, reeking with blood, in contrast to her little island where petty larceny was about the standard of current misdeeds, with, now and then, some more pronounced crime – and that only amongst the imported coolie labourers on sugar estates or the Negroes of the town. But in Europe these things were being done daily by a wicked population of white men amongst whom, as that ruffianly, aristocratic old Miss Jacobus pointed out, the wandering sailors, the associates of her precious papa, were the lowest of the low.

It was impossible to give her a sense of proportion. I suppose she figured England to herself as about the size of the Pearl of the Ocean, in which case it would certainly have been reeking with gore and a mere wreck of burgled houses from end to end. One could not make her understand that these horrors on which she fed her imagination were lost in the mass of orderly life like a few drops of blood in the ocean. She directed upon me for a moment the uncomprehending glance of her narrowed eyes and then would turn her scornful powdered face away without a word. She would not even take the trouble to shrug her shoulders.

At that time the batches of papers brought by the last mail reported a series of crimes in the East End of London, there was a sensational case of abduction in France and a fine display of armed robbery in Australia. One afternoon crossing the dining room I heard Miss Jacobus piping in the verandah with venomous animosity, 'I don't know what your precious papa is plotting with that fellow. But he's just the sort of man who's capable of carrying you off far away somewhere and then cutting your throat some day for your money.'

There was a good half of the length of the verandah between their chairs. I came out and sat down fiercely midway between them.

'Yes, that's what we do with girls in Europe,' I began in a grimly matter-of-fact tone. I think Miss Jacobus was disconcerted by my sudden appearance. I turned upon her with cold ferocity: 'As to objectionable old women, they are first strangled quietly, then cut up into small pieces and thrown away, a bit here and a bit there. They vanish – '

I cannot go so far as to say I had terrified her. But she was troubled by my truculence, the more so because I had been always addressing her with a politeness she did not deserve. Her plump, knitting hands fell slowly on her knees. She said not a word while I fixed her with severe determination. Then as I turned away from her at last, she laid down her work gently and, with noiseless movements, retreated from the verandah. In fact, she vanished.

But I was not thinking of her. I was looking at the girl. It was what I was coming for daily; troubled, ashamed, eager; finding in my nearness to her a unique sensation that I indulged with dread, self-contempt, and deep pleasure, as if it were a secret vice bound to end in my undoing, like the habit of some drug or other that ruins and degrades its slave.

I looked her over, from the top of her dishevelled head, down the lovely line of the shoulder, following the curve of the hip, the draped form of the long limb, right down to her fine ankle below a torn, soiled flounce, and as far as the point of the shabby, high-heeled, blue slipper, dangling from her well-shaped foot, which she moved slightly, with quick, nervous jerks, as if impatient of my presence. And in the scent of the massed flowers I seemed to breathe her special and inexplicable charm, the heady perfume of the everlastingly irritated captive of the garden.

I looked at her rounded chin, the Jacobus chin; at the full, red lips pouting in the powdered, sallow face; at the firm modelling of the cheek, the grains of white in the hairs of the straight sombre eyebrows; at the long eyes, a narrowed gleam of liquid white and intense motionless black, with their gaze so empty of thought, and so absorbed in their fixity that she seemed to be staring at her own lonely image, in some far-off mirror hidden from my sight amongst the trees.

And suddenly, without looking at me, with the appearance of a person speaking to herself, she asked, in that voice slightly harsh yet mellow and always irritated, 'Why do you keep on coming here?'

'Why do I keep on coming here?' I repeated, taken by surprise. I could not have told her. I could not even tell myself with sincerity why I was coming there. 'What's the good of you asking a question like that?'

'Nothing is any good,' she observed scornfully to the empty air, her chin propped on her hand, that hand never extended to any man, that no one had ever grasped – for I had only grasped her shoulder once – that generous, fine, somewhat masculine hand. I knew well the peculiarly efficient shape – broad at the base, tapering at the fingers – of that hand, for which there was nothing in the world to lay hold of. I pretended to be playful.

'No! But do you really care to know?'

She shrugged indolently her magnificent shoulders, from which the dingy thin wrapper was slipping a little.

'Oh – never mind – never mind!'

There was something smouldering under those airs of lassitude. She exasperated me by the provocation of her nonchalance, by something elusive and defiant in her very form that I wanted to seize. I said roughly, 'Why? Don't you think I should tell you the truth?'

Her eyes glided my way for a sidelong look, and she murmured, moving only her full, pouting lips, 'I think you would not dare.'

'Do you imagine I am afraid of you? What on earth... Well, it's possible, after all, that I don't know exactly why I am coming here. Let us say, with Miss Jacobus, that it is for no good. You seem to believe the outrageous things she says, if you do have a row with her now and then.'

She snapped out viciously: 'Who else am I to believe?

'I don't know,' I had to own, seeing her suddenly very helpless and condemned to moral solitude by the verdict of a respectable community. 'You might believe me, if you chose.'

She made a slight movement and asked me at once, with an effort as if making an experiment, 'What is the business between you and papa?'

'Don't you know the nature of your father's business? Come! He sells provisions to ships.'

She became rigid again in her crouching pose.

'Not that. What brings you here – to this house?'

'And suppose it's you? You would not call that business? Would you? And now let us drop the subject. It's no use. My ship will be ready for sea the day after tomorrow.'

She murmured a distinctly scared 'So soon', and getting up quickly, went to the little table and poured herself a glass of water. She walked with rapid steps and with an indolent swaying of her whole young figure above the hips; when she passed near me I felt with tenfold force the charm of the peculiar, promising sensation I had formed the habit to seek near her. I thought with sudden dismay that this was the end of it; that after one more day I would be no longer able to come into this verandah, sit on this chair, and taste perversely the flavour of contempt in her indolent poses, drink in the provocation of her scornful looks, and listen to the curt, insolent remarks uttered in that harsh and seductive voice. As if my innermost nature had been altered by the action of some moral poison, I felt an abject dread of going to sea.

I had to exercise a sudden self-control, as one puts on a brake, to prevent myself jumping up to stride about, shout, gesticulate, make her a scene. What for? What about? I had no idea. It was just the relief of violence that I wanted, and I lolled back in my chair, trying to keep my lips formed in a smile; that half-indulgent, half-mocking smile that was my shield against the shafts of her contempt and the insulting sallies flung at me by the old woman.

She drank the water at a draught, with the avidity of raging thirst, and let herself fall on the nearest chair, as if utterly overcome. Her attitude, like certain tones of her voice, had in it something masculine: the knees apart in the ample wrapper, the clasped hands hanging between them, her body leaning forward, with drooping head. I stared at the heavy black coil of twisted hair. It was enormous, crowning the bowed head with a crushing and disdained glory. The escaped wisps hung straight

58

down. And suddenly I perceived that the girl was trembling from head to foot, as though that glass of iced water had chilled her to the bone.

'What's the matter now?' I said, startled, but in no very sympathetic mood.

She shook her bowed, overweighted head and cried in a stifled voice but with a rising inflection: 'Go away! Go away! Go away!'

I got up then and approached her, with a strange sort of anxiety. I looked down at her round, strong neck, then stooped low enough to peep at her face. And I began to tremble a little myself.

'What on earth are you gone wild about, Miss Don't Care?'

She flung herself backwards violently, her head going over the back of the chair. And now it was her smooth, full, palpitating throat that lay exposed to my bewildered stare. Her eyes were nearly closed, with only a horrible white gleam under the lids as if she were dead.

'What has come to you?' I asked in awe. 'What are you terrifying yourself with?'

She pulled herself together, her eyes open frightfully wide now. The tropical afternoon was lengthening the shadows on the hot, weary earth, the abode of obscure desires, of extravagant hopes, of unimaginable terrors.

'Never mind! Don't care!' Then, after a gasp, she spoke with such frightful rapidity that I could hardly make out the amazing words: 'For if you were to shut me up in an empty place as smooth all round as the palm of my hand, I could always strangle myself with my hair.'

For a moment, doubting my ears, I let this inconceivable declaration sink into me. It is ever impossible to guess at the wild thoughts that pass through the heads of our fellow creatures. What monstrous imaginings of violence could have dwelt under the low forehead of that girl who had been taught to regard her father as 'capable of anything' more in the light of a misfortune than that of a disgrace; as, evidently, something to be resented and feared rather than to be ashamed of? She seemed, indeed, as unaware of shame as of anything else in the world; but in her ignorance, her resentment and fear took a childish and violent shape.

Of course she spoke without knowing the value of words. What could she know of death – she who knew nothing of life? It was merely as the proof of her being beside herself with some odious apprehension that this extraordinary speech had moved me, not to pity, but to a fascinated, horrified wonder. I had no idea what notion she had of her danger. Some sort of abduction. It was quite possible with the talk of that atrocious old woman. Perhaps she thought she could be carried off, bound hand and foot and even gagged. At that surmise I felt as if the door of a furnace had been opened in front of me.

'Upon my honour!' I cried. 'You shall end by going crazy if you listen to that abominable old aunt of yours – '

I studied her haggard expression, her trembling lips. Her cheeks even seemed sunk a little. But how I, the associate of her disreputable father, the 'lowest of the low' from the criminal Europe, could manage to reassure her I had no conception. She was exasperating.

'Heavens and earth! What do you think I can do?'

'I don't know.'

Her chin certainly trembled. And she was looking at me with extreme attention. I made a step nearer to her chair.

'I shall do nothing. I promise you that. Will that do? Do you understand? I shall do nothing whatever, of any kind, and the day after tomorrow I shall be gone.'

What else could I have said? She seemed to drink in my words with the thirsty avidity with which she had emptied the glass of water. She whispered tremulously, in that touching tone I had heard once before on her lips, and which thrilled me again with the same emotion, 'I would believe you. But what about papa – '

'He be hanged!' My emotion betrayed itself by the brutality of my tone. 'I've had enough of your papa. Are you so stupid as to imagine that I am frightened of him? He can't make me do anything.'

All that sounded feeble to me in the face of her ignorance. But I must conclude that the 'accent of sincerity' has, as some people say, a really irresistible power. The effect was far beyond my hopes – and even beyond my conception. To watch the change in the girl was like watching a miracle – the gradual but swift relaxation of her tense glance, of her stiffened muscles, of every fibre of her body. That black, fixed stare into which I had read a tragic meaning more than once, in which I had found a sombre seduction, was perfectly empty now, void of all consciousness whatever, and not even aware any longer of my presence; it had become a little sleepy, in the Jacobus fashion.

But, man being a perverse animal, instead of rejoicing at my complete success, I beheld it with astounded and indignant eyes. There was something cynical in that unconcealed alteration, the true Jacobus shamelessness. I felt as though I had been cheated in some rather complicated deal into which I had entered against my better judgement. Yes, cheated without any regard for, at least, the forms of decency.

With an easy, indolent, and in its indolence supple, feline movement, she rose from the chair, so provokingly ignoring me now, that for very rage I held my ground within less than a foot of her. Leisurely and tranquil, behaving right before me with the ease of a person alone in a room, she extended her beautiful arms, with her hands clenched, her body swaying, her head thrown back a little, revelling contemptuously in a sense of relief, easing her limbs in freedom after all these days of crouching, motionless poses when she had been so furious and so afraid.

All this with supreme indifference, incredible, offensive, exasperating, like ingratitude doubled with treachery.

I ought to have been flattered, perhaps, but, on the contrary, my anger grew; her movement to pass by me as if I were a wooden post or a piece of furniture, that unconcerned movement brought it to a head.

I won't say I did not know what I was doing, but, certainly, cool reflection had nothing to do with the circumstance that next moment both my arms were round her waist. It was an impulsive action, as one snatches at something falling or escaping, and it had no hypocritical gentleness about it either. She had no time to make a sound, and the first kiss I planted on her closed lips was vicious enough to have been a bite.

She did not resist, and of course I did not stop at one. She let me go on, not as if she were inanimate – I felt her there, close against me, young, full of vigour, of life, a strong desirable creature, but as if she did not care in the least, in the absolute assurance of her safety, what I did or left undone. Our faces brought close together in this storm of haphazard caresses, her big, black, wide-open eyes looked into mine without the girl appearing either angry or pleased or moved in any way. In that steady gaze that seemed impersonally to watch my madness I could detect a slight surprise, perhaps – nothing more. I showered kisses upon her face and there did not seem to be any reason why this should not go on for ever.

That thought flashed through my head, and I was on the point of desisting, when, all at once, she began to struggle with a sudden violence that all but freed her instantly, which revived my exasperation with her, indeed a fierce desire never to let her go any more. I tightened my embrace in time, gasping out, 'No – you don't!' as if she were my mortal enemy. On her part not a word was said. Putting her hands against my chest, she pushed with all her might without succeeding to break the circle of my arms. Except that she seemed thoroughly awake now, her eyes gave me no clue whatever. To meet her black stare was like looking into a deep well, and I was totally unprepared for her change of tactics. Instead of trying to tear my hands apart, she flung herself upon my breast and with a downward, undulating, serpentine motion, a quick sliding dive, she got away from me smoothly. It was all very swift; I saw her pick up the tail of her wrapper and run for the door at the end of the verandah not very gracefully. She appeared to be limping a little – and then she vanished; the door swung behind her so noiselessly that I could not believe it was completely closed. I had a distinct suspicion of her black eye being at the crack to watch what I would do. I could not make up my mind whether to shake my fist in that direction or blow a kiss.

6

Either would have been perfectly consistent with my feelings. I gazed at the door, hesitating, but in the end I did neither. The monition of some sixth sense – the sense of guilt, maybe, that sense that always acts too late, alas! – warned me to look round, and at once I became aware that the conclusion of this tumultuous episode was likely to be a matter of lively anxiety. Jacobus was standing in the doorway of the dining room. How long he had been there it was impossible to guess, and remembering my struggle with the girl I thought he must have been its mute witness from beginning to end. But this supposition seemed almost incredible. Perhaps that impenetrable girl had heard him come in and had got away in time.

He stepped on to the verandah in his usual manner, heavy-eyed, with glued lips. I marvelled at the girl's resemblance to this man. Those long, Egyptian eyes, that low forehead of a stupid goddess, she had found in the sawdust of the circus, but all the rest of the face, the design and the modelling, the rounded chin, the very lips – all that was Jacobus, fined down, more finished, more expressive.

His thick hand fell on and grasped with force the back of a light chair (there were several standing about) and I perceived the chance of a broken head at the end of all this – most likely. My mortification was extreme. The scandal would be horrible; that was unavoidable. But how to act so as to satisfy myself I did not know. I stood on my guard and at any rate faced him. There was nothing else for it. Of one thing I was certain, that, however brazen my attitude, it could never equal the characteristic Jacobus impudence.

He gave me his melancholy, glued smile and sat down. I own I was relieved. The perspective of passing from kisses to blows had nothing particularly attractive in it. Perhaps – perhaps he had seen nothing? He behaved as usual, but he had never before found me alone on the verandah. If he had alluded to it, if he had asked, 'Where's Alice?' or something of the sort, I would have been able to judge from the tone. He would give me no opportunity. The striking peculiarity was that he had never looked up at me yet. 'He knows,' I said to myself confidently. And my contempt for him relieved my disgust with myself.

'You are early home,' I remarked.

'Things are very quiet; nothing doing at the store today,' he explained with a cast-down air.

'Oh, well, you know, I am off,' I said, feeling that this, perhaps, was the best thing to do.

'Yes,' he breathed out. 'Day after tomorrow.'

This was not what I had meant, but as he gazed persistently on the floor, I followed the direction of his glance. In the absolute stillness of the house we stared at the high-heeled slipper the girl had lost in her flight. We stared. It lay overturned.

After what seemed a very long time to me, Jacobus hitched his chair forward, stooped with extended arm and picked it up. It looked a slender thing in his big, thick hands. It was not really a slipper, but a low shoe of blue, glazed kid, rubbed and shabby. It had straps to go over the instep, but the girl only thrust her feet in, after her slovenly manner. Jacobus raised his eyes from the shoe to look at me.

'Sit down, Captain,' he said at last, in his subdued tone.

As if the sight of that shoe had renewed the spell, I gave up suddenly the idea of leaving the house there and then. It had become impossible. I sat down, keeping my eyes on the fascinating object. Jacobus turned his daughter's shoe over and over in his cushioned paws as if studying the way the thing was made. He contemplated the thin sole for a time; then glancing inside with an absorbed air: 'I am glad I found you here, Captain.'

I answered this by some sort of grunt, watching him covertly. Then I added: 'You won't have much more of me now.'

He was still deep in the interior of that shoe on which my eyes too were resting.

'Have you thought any more of this deal in potatoes I spoke to you about the other day?'

'No, I haven't,' I answered curtly. He checked my movement to rise by an austere, commanding gesture of the hand holding that fatal shoe. I remained seated and glared at him. 'You know I don't trade.'

'You ought to, Captain. You ought to.'

I reflected. If I left that house now I would never see the girl again. And I felt I must see her once more, if only for an instant. It was a need, not to be reasoned with, not to be disregarded.

No, I did not want to go away. I wanted to stay for one more experience of that strange provoking sensation and of indefinite desire, the habit of which had made me – me of all people! – dread the prospect of going to sea.

'Mr Jacobus,' I pronounced slowly. 'Do you really think that upon the whole and taking various matters into consideration – I mean everything, do you understand? – it would be a good thing for me to trade, let us say, with you?'

I waited for a while. He went on looking at the shoe that he held now crushed in the middle, the worn point of the toe and the high heel protruding on each side of his heavy fist.

'That will be all right,' he said, facing me squarely at last.

'Are you sure?'

'You'll find it quite correct, Captain.' He had uttered his habitual phrases in his usual placid, breath-saving voice and stood my hard, inquisitive stare sleepily without as much as a wink.

'Then let us trade,' I said, turning my shoulder to him. 'I see you are bent on it.'

I did not want an open scandal, but I thought that outward decency may be bought too dearly at times. I included Jacobus, myself, the whole population of the island, in the same contemptuous disgust as though we had been partners in an ignoble transaction. And the remembered vision at sea, diaphanous and blue, of the Pearl of the Ocean at sixty miles off, the unsubstantial, clear marvel of it as if evoked by the art of a beautiful and pure magic, turned into a thing of horrors too. Was this the fortune this vaporous and rare apparition had held for me in its hard heart, hidden within the shape as of fair dreams and mist? Was this my luck?

'I think' – Jacobus became suddenly audible after what seemed the silence of vile meditation – 'that you might conveniently take some thirty tons. That would be about the lot, Captain.'

'Would it? The lot! I dare say it would be convenient, but I haven't got enough money for that.'

I had never seen him so animated.

'No!' he exclaimed with what I took for the accent of grim menace. 'That's a pity.' He paused, then, unrelenting: 'How much money have you got, Captain?' he enquired with awful directness.

It was my turn to face him squarely. I did so and mentioned the amount I could dispose of. And I perceived that he was disappointed. He thought it over, his calculating gaze lost in mine, for quite a long time before he came out in a thoughtful tone with the rapacious suggestion: 'You could draw some more from your charterers. That would be quite easy, Captain.'

'No, I couldn't,' I retorted brusquely. 'I've drawn my salary up to date, and besides, the ship's accounts are closed.'

I was growing furious. I pursued: 'And I'll tell you what: if I could do it I wouldn't.' Then throwing off all restraint, I added, 'You are a bit too much of a Jacobus, Mr Jacobus.'

The tone alone was insulting enough, but he remained tranquil, only a little puzzled, till something seemed to dawn upon him; but the unwonted light in his eyes died out instantly. As a Jacobus on his native heath, what a mere skipper chose to say could not touch him, outcast as he was. As a ship-chandler he could stand anything. All I caught of his mumble was a vague – 'quite correct', than which nothing could have been more egregiously false at bottom – to my view, at least. But I remembered – I had never forgotten – that I must see the girl. I did not mean to go. I meant to stay in the house till I had seen her once more.

'Look here!' I said finally. 'I'll tell you what I'll do. I'll take as many of your confounded potatoes as my money will buy, on condition that you go off at once down to the wharf to see them loaded in the lighter and sent alongside the ship straight away.

Take the invoice and a signed receipt with you. Here's the key of my desk. Give it to Burns. He will pay you.'

He got up from his chair before I had finished speaking, but he refused to take the key. Burns would never do it. He wouldn't like to ask him even.

'Well, then,' I said, eyeing him slightingly, 'there's nothing for it, Mr Jacobus, but you must wait on board till I come off to settle with you.'

'That will be all right, Captain. I will go at once.'

He seemed at a loss what to do with the girl's shoe he was still holding in his fist. Finally, looking dully at me, he put it down on the chair from which he had risen.

'And you, Captain? Won't you come along, too, just to see –'

'Don't bother about me. I'll take care of myself.'

He remained perplexed for a moment, as if trying to understand, and then his weighty 'Certainly, certainly, Captain' seemed to be the outcome of some sudden thought. His big chest heaved. Was it a sigh? As he went out to hurry off those potatoes he never looked back at me.

I waited till the noise of his footsteps had died out of the dining room, and I waited a little longer. Then turning towards the distant door I raised my voice along the verandah: 'Alice!'

Nothing answered me, not even a stir behind the door. Jacobus' house might have been made empty for me to make myself at home in. I did not call again. I had become aware of a great discouragement. I was mentally jaded, morally dejected. I turned to the garden again, sitting down with my elbows spread on the low balustrade, and took my head in my hands.

The evening closed upon me. The shadows lengthened, deepened, mingled together into a pool of twilight in which the flower-beds glowed like coloured embers; whiffs of heavy scent came to me as if the dusk of this hemisphere were but the dimness of a temple and the garden an enormous censer swinging before the altar of the stars. The colours of the blossoms deepened, losing their glow one by one.

The girl, when I turned my head at a slight noise, appeared to me very tall and slender, advancing with a swaying limp, a floating and uneven motion that ended in the sinking of her shadowy form into the deep low chair. And I don't know why or whence I received the impression that she had come too late. She ought to have appeared at my call. She ought to have... It was as if a supreme opportunity had been missed.

I rose and took a seat close to her, nearly opposite her armchair. Her ever discontented voice addressed me at once, contemptuously: 'You are still here.'

I pitched mine low.

'You have come out at last.'

'I came to look for my shoe – before they bring in the lights.'

It was her harsh, enticing whisper, subdued, not very steady, but its low tremulousness gave me no thrill now. I could only make out the oval of her face, her uncovered throat, the long, white gleam of her eyes. She was mysterious enough. Her hands were resting on the arms of the chair. But where was the mysterious and provoking sensation that was like the perfume of her flower-like youth? I said quietly, 'I have got your shoe here.' She made no sound and I continued, 'You had better give me your foot and I will put it on for you.'

She made no movement. I bent low down and groped for her foot under the flounces of the wrapper. She did not withdraw it and I put on the shoe, buttoning the instep-strap. It was an inanimate foot. I lowered it gently to the floor.

'If you buttoned the strap you would not be losing your shoe, Miss Don't Care,' I said, trying to be playful without conviction. I felt more like wailing over the lost illusion of vague desire, over the sudden conviction that I would never find again near her the strange, half-evil, half-tender sensation that had given its acrid flavour to so many days, which had made her appear tragic and promising, pitiful and provoking. That was all over.

'Your father picked it up,' I said, thinking she may just as well be told of the fact.

'I am not afraid of papa – by himself,' she declared scornfully.

'Oh! It's only in conjunction with his disreputable associates, strangers, the "riff-raff of Europe" as your charming aunt or great-aunt says – men like me, for instance – that you – '

'I am not afraid of you,' she snapped out.

'That's because you don't know that I am now doing business with your father. Yes, I am in fact doing exactly what he wants me to do. I've broken my promise to you. That's the sort of man I am. And now – aren't you afraid? If you believe what that dear, kind, truthful old lady says you ought to be.'

It was with unexpected modulated softness that she affirmed: 'No. I am not afraid.' She hesitated... 'Not now.'

'Quite right. You needn't be. I shall not see you again before I go to sea.' I rose and stood near her chair. 'But I shall often think of you in this old garden, passing under the trees over there, walking between these gorgeous flower-beds. You must love this garden – '

'I love nothing.'

I heard in her sullen tone the faint echo of that resentfully tragic note that I had found once so provoking. But it left me unmoved except for a sudden and weary conviction of the emptiness of all things under Heaven.

'Goodbye, Alice,' I said.

She did not answer, she did not move. To merely take her hand, shake it, and go away seemed impossible, almost improper. I stooped without haste and pressed my lips to her smooth fore-head. This was the moment when I realised clearly with a sort of terror my complete detachment from that unfortunate creature.

And as I lingered in that cruel self-knowledge I felt the light touch of her arms falling languidly on my neck and received a hasty, awkward, haphazard kiss that missed my lips. No! She was not afraid, but I was no longer moved. Her arms slipped off my neck slowly, she made no sound, the deep wicker armchair creaked slightly; only a sense of my dignity prevented me fleeing headlong from that catastrophic revelation.

I traversed the dining room slowly. I thought: She's listening to my footsteps; she can't help it; she'll hear me open and shut that door. And I closed it as gently behind me as if I had been a thief retreating with his ill-gotten booty. During that stealthy act I experienced the last touch of emotion in that house, at the thought of the girl I had left sitting there in the obscurity, with her heavy hair and empty eyes as black as the night itself, staring into the walled garden, silent, warm, odorous with the perfume of imprisoned flowers, which, like herself, were lost to sight in a world buried in darkness.

The narrow, ill-lighted, rustic streets I knew so well on my way to the harbour were extremely quiet. I felt in my heart that the further one ventures the better one understands how everything in our life is common, short, and empty; that it is in seeking the unknown in our sensations that we discover how mediocre are our attempts and how soon defeated! Jacobus' boatman was waiting at the steps with an unusual air of readiness. He put me alongside the ship, but did not give me his confidential 'Good evening, sah,' and, instead of shoving off at once, remained holding by the ladder.

I was a thousand miles from commercial affairs, when on the dark quarterdeck Mr Burns positively rushed at me, stammering with excitement. He had been pacing the deck distractedly for hours awaiting my arrival. Just before sunset a lighter loaded with potatoes had come alongside with that fat ship-chandler himself sitting on the pile of sacks. He was now stuck immovable in the cabin. What was the meaning of it all? Surely I did not –

'Yes, Mr Burns, I did,' I cut him short. He was beginning to make gestures of despair when I stopped that, too, by giving him the key of my desk and desiring him, in a tone that admitted of no argument, to go below at once, pay Mr Jacobus' bill, and send him out of the ship.

'I don't want to see him,' I confessed frankly, climbing the poop ladder. I felt extremely tired. Dropping on the seat of the skylight, I gave myself up to idle gazing at the lights about the quay and at the black mass of the mountain on the south side of the harbour. I never heard Jacobus leave the ship with every single sovereign of my ready cash in his pocket. I never heard anything till, a long time afterwards, Mr Burns, unable to contain himself any longer, intruded upon me with his ridiculously angry lamentations at my weakness and good nature.

'Of course, there's plenty of room in the afterhatch. But they are sure to go rotten down there. Well! I never heard... seventeen tons! I suppose I must hoist in that lot first thing tomorrow morning.'

'I suppose you must. Unless you drop them overboard. But I'm afraid you can't do that. I wouldn't mind myself, but it's forbidden to throw rubbish into the harbour, you know.'

'That is the truest word you have said for many a day, sir – rubbish. That's just what I expect they are. Nearly eighty good gold sovereigns gone; a perfectly clean sweep of your drawer, sir. Bless me if I understand!'

As it was impossible to throw the right light on this commercial transaction I left him to his lamentations and under the impression that I was a hopeless fool. Next day I did not go ashore. For one thing, I had no money to go ashore with – no, not enough to buy a cigarette. Jacobus had made a clean sweep. But that was not the only reason. The Pearl of the Ocean had in a few short hours grown odious to me. And I did not want to meet any one. My reputation had suffered. I knew I was the object of unkind and sarcastic comments.

The following morning at sunrise, just as our sternfasts had been let go and the tug plucked us out from between the buoys, I saw Jacobus standing up in his boat. The nigger was pulling hard; several baskets of provisions for ships were stowed between the thwarts. The father of Alice was going his morning round. His countenance was tranquil and friendly. He raised his arm and shouted something with great heartiness. But his voice was of the sort that doesn't carry any distance; all I could catch faintly, or rather guess at, were the words 'next time' and 'quite correct'. And it was only of these last that I was certain. Raising my arm perfunctorily for all response, I turned away. I rather resented the familiarity of the thing. Hadn't I settled accounts finally with him by means of that potato bargain?

This being a harbour story it is not my purpose to speak of our passage. I was glad enough to be at sea, but not with the gladness of old days. Formerly I had no memories to take away with me. I shared in the blessed forgetfulness of sailors, that forgetfulness natural and invincible, which resembles innocence in so far that it prevents self-examination. Now however I remembered the girl. During the first few days I was forever questioning myself as to the nature of facts and sensations connected with her person and with my conduct.

And I must say also that Mr Burns's intolerable fussing with those potatoes was not calculated to make me forget the part that I had played. He looked upon it as a purely commercial transaction of a particularly foolish kind, and his devotion – if it was devotion and not mere cussedness as I came to regard it before long – inspired him with a zeal to minimise my loss as much as possible. Oh, yes! He took care of those infamous potatoes with a vengeance, as the saying goes.

Everlastingly, there was a tackle over the afterhatch and everlastingly the watch on deck were pulling up, spreading out, picking over, rebagging, and lowering down again, some part of that lot of potatoes. My bargain with all its remotest associations, mental and visual – the garden of flowers and scents, the girl with her provoking contempt and her tragic loneliness of a hopeless castaway – was everlastingly dangled before my eyes, for thousands of miles along the open sea. And as if by a satanic refinement of irony it was accompanied by a most awful smell. Whiffs from decaying potatoes pursued me on the poop, they mingled with my thoughts, with my food, poisoned my very dreams. They made an atmosphere of corruption for the ship.

I remonstrated with Mr Burns about this excessive care. I would have been well content to batten the hatch down and let them perish under the deck.

That perhaps would have been unsafe. The horrid emanations might have flavoured the cargo of sugar. They seemed strong enough to taint the very ironwork. In addition Mr Burns made it a personal matter. He assured me he knew how to treat a cargo of potatoes at sea – had been in the trade as a boy, he said. He meant to make my loss as small as possible. What between his devotion – it must have been devotion – and his vanity, I positively dared not give him the order to throw my commercial venture overboard. I believe he would have refused point blank to obey my lawful command. An unprecedented and comical situation would have been created with which I did not feel equal to deal.

I welcomed the coming of bad weather as no sailor had ever done. When at last I hove the ship to, to pick up the pilot outside Port Philip Heads, the afterhatch had not been opened for more than a week and I might have believed that no such thing as a potato had ever been on board.

It was an abominable day, raw, blustering, with great squalls of wind and rain; the pilot, a cheery person, looked after the ship and chatted to me, streaming from head to foot; and the heavier the lash of the downpour the more pleased with himself and everything around him he seemed to be. He rubbed his wet hands with a satisfaction, which to me, who had stood that kind of thing for several days and nights, seemed inconceivable in any non-aquatic creature.

'You seem to enjoy getting wet, Pilot,' I remarked.

He had a bit of land round his house in the suburbs and it was of his garden he was thinking. At the sound of the word garden, unheard, unspoken for so many days, I had a vision of gorgeous colour, of sweet scents, of a girlish figure crouching in a chair. Yes. That was a distinct emotion breaking into the peace I had found in the sleepless anxieties of my responsibility during a week of dangerous bad weather. The Colony, the pilot explained, had suffered from unparalleled drought. This was the first decent drop of water they had had for seven months. The root crops were lost. And, trying to be casual, but with visible interest, he asked me if I had perchance any potatoes to spare.

Potatoes! I had managed to forget them. In a moment I felt plunged into corruption up to my neck. Mr Burns was making eyes at me behind the pilot's back.

Finally, he obtained a ton, and paid ten pounds for it. This was twice the price of my bargain with Jacobus. The spirit of covetousness woke up in me. That night, in harbour, before I slept, the Custom House galley came alongside. While his underlings were putting seals on the storerooms, the officer in charge took me aside confidentially. 'I say, Captain, you don't happen to have any potatoes to sell.'

Clearly there was a potato famine in the land. I let him have a ton for twelve pounds and he went away joyfully. That night

I dreamt of a pile of gold in the form of a grave in which a girl was buried, and woke up callous with greed. On calling at my shipbroker's office, that man, after the usual business had been transacted, pushed his spectacles up on his forehead.

'I was thinking, Captain, that coming from the Pearl of the Ocean you may have some potatoes to sell.'

I said negligently, 'Oh, yes, I could spare you a ton. Fifteen pounds.'

He exclaimed, 'I say!' But after studying my face for a while accepted my terms with a faint grimace. It seems that these people could not exist without potatoes. I could. I didn't want to see a potato as long as I lived, but the demon of lucre had taken possession of me. How the news got about I don't know, but, returning on board rather late, I found a small group of men of the coster type hanging about the waist, while Mr Burns walked to and fro the quarterdeck loftily, keeping a triumphant eye on them. They had come to buy potatoes.

'These chaps have been waiting here in the sun for hours,' Burns whispered to me excitedly. 'They have drank the water cask dry. Don't you throw away your chances, sir. You are too good-natured.'

I selected a man with thick legs and a man with a cast in his eye to negotiate with, simply because they were easily distinguishable from the rest. 'You have the money on you?' I enquired, before taking them down into the cabin.

'Yes, sir,' they answered in one voice, slapping their pockets. I liked their air of quiet determination. Long before the end of the day all the potatoes were sold at about three times the price I had paid for them. Mr Burns, feverish and exulting, congratulated himself on his skilful care of my commercial venture, but hinted plainly that I ought to have made more of it.

That night I did not sleep very well. I thought of Jacobus by fits and starts, between snatches of dreams concerned with castaways starving on a desert island covered with flowers. It was extremely unpleasant. In the morning, tired and unrefreshed, I sat down and wrote a long letter to my owners, giving them a carefully thought-out scheme for the ship's employment in the East and about the China Seas for the next two years. I spent the day at that task and felt somewhat more at peace when it was done.

Their reply came in due course. They were greatly struck with my project, but considering that, notwithstanding the unfortunate difficulty with the bags (which they trusted I would know how to guard against in the future), the voyage showed a very fair profit, they thought it would be better to keep the ship in the sugar trade – at least for the present.

I turned over the page and read on:

We have had a letter from our good friend Mr Jacobus. We are pleased to see how well you have hit it off with him; for, not to speak of his assistance in the unfortunate matter of the bags, he writes us that should you, by using all possible dispatch, manage to bring the ship back early in the season he would be able to give us a good rate of freight. We have no doubt that your best endeavours... etc.... etc.

I dropped the letter and sat motionless for a long time. Then I wrote my answer (it was a short one) and went ashore myself to post it. But I passed one letterbox, then another, and in the end found myself going up Collins Street with the letter still in my pocket – against my heart. Collins Street at four o'clock in the afternoon is not exactly a desert solitude, but I had never felt more isolated from the rest of mankind as when I walked that day its crowded pavement, battling desperately with my thoughts and feeling already vanquished.

There came a moment when the awful tenacity of Jacobus, the man of one passion and of one idea, appeared to me almost heroic. He had not given me up. He had gone again to his odious brother. And then he appeared to me odious himself. Was it for his own sake or for the sake of the poor girl? And on that last supposition the memory of the kiss that missed my lips appalled me, for whatever he had seen, or guessed at, or risked, he knew nothing of that. Unless the girl had told him. How could I go back to fan that fatal spark with my cold breath? No, no, that unexpected kiss had to be paid for at its full price.

At the first letterbox I came to I stopped and reaching into my breast pocket I took out the letter – it was as if I were plucking out my very heart – and dropped it through the slit. Then I went straight on board.

I wondered what dreams I would have that night, but as it turned out I did not sleep at all. At breakfast I informed Mr Burns that I had resigned my command.

He dropped his knife and fork and looked at me with indignation.

'You have, sir! I thought you loved the ship.'

'So I do, Burns,' I said. 'But the fact is that the Indian Ocean and everything that is in it has lost its charm for me. I am going home as passenger by the Suez Canal.'

'Everything that is in it,' he repeated angrily. 'I've never heard anybody talk like this. And to tell you the truth, sir, all the time we have been together I've never quite made you out. What's one ocean more than another? Charm, indeed!'

He was really devoted to me, I believe. But he cheered up when I told him that I had recommended him for my successor.

'Anyhow,' he remarked, 'let people say what they like, this Jacobus has served your turn. I must admit that this potato business has paid extremely well. Of course, if only you had –'

'Yes, Mr Burns,' I interrupted. 'Quite a smile of fortune.'

But I could not tell him that it was driving me out of the ship I had learned to love. And as I sat heavy-hearted at that parting,

seeing all my plans destroyed, my modest future endangered –
for this command was like a foot in the stirrup for a young man
– he gave up completely for the first time his critical attitude.

'A wonderful piece of luck!' he said.

Biographical note

Joseph Conrad was born Józef Teodor Konrad Korzeniowski to Polish parents in Berdichev in the Ukraine in 1857. His father, a landless gentleman, poet, and translator of English, French and German literature, was active in the Polish patriotic underground, which resulted in his imprisonment and his family's exile to Volagda in northern Russia and later in the eastern Ukraine. There, in Chernihiv, Conrad's mother died in 1867. Once released from exile, his father soon died of tuberculosis, and, from 1869, Conrad was supported by his uncle, Tadeusz Bobrowski. After school in Kraków, Conrad persuaded Bobrowski to let him join the French merchant marine with whom he was to travel to the West Indies several times between 1875 and 1878. His career continued in the British merchant marine, where he rose from common seaman to first mate, obtaining his master mariner's certificate, and, in 1886, command of his own vessel, *Otago*. (It was also in 1886, that Conrad became a British subject.) His following years at sea were to prove vastly influential on his writing, as he sailed all over the world, and, most famously, up the Congo river in 1890, a journey depicted in his tale, *Heart of Darkness* (written 1899, published 1902).

Conrad settled in England in 1894, and married Jessie George in 1896, having published his first novel, *Almayer's Folly*, in 1895. Writing in his third language, a language he did not learn until aged twenty, Conrad did not achieve financial and popular success until *Chance* (1913), although earlier works such as *Nostromo* (1904), *The Secret Agent* (1904), and *Under Western Eyes* (1911) are held in greater critical esteem. Joseph Conrad died in 1924, and, after a brief period of neglect, was declared by F.R. Leavis in 1941 as 'among the very greatest novelists in the language'.

HESPERUS PRESS

Hesperus Press, as suggested by the Latin motto, is committed to bringing near what is far – far both in space and time. Works written by the greatest authors, and unjustly neglected or simply little known in the English-speaking world, are made accessible through new translations and a completely fresh editorial approach. Through these classic works, the reader is introduced to the greatest writers from all times and all cultures.

For more information on Hesperus Press, please visit our website: **www.hesperuspress.com**

ET REMOTISSIMA PROPE

SELECTED TITLES FROM HESPERUS PRESS

Author	Title	Foreword writer
Mikhail Bulgakov	*A Dog's Heart*	A.S. Byatt
Mikhail Bulgakov	*The Fatal Eggs*	Doris Lessing
Anthony Burgess	*The Eve of St Venus*	
Colette	*Claudine's House*	Doris Lessing
Marie Ferranti	*The Princess of Mantua*	
Beppe Fenoglio	*A Private Affair*	Paul Bailey
F. Scott Fitzgerald	*The Popular Girl*	Helen Dunmore
F. Scott Fitzgerald	*The Rich Boy*	John Updike
Graham Greene	*No Man's Land*	David Lodge
Franz Kafka	*Metamorphosis*	Martin Jarvis
Franz Kafka	*The Trial*	Zadie Smith
D.H. Lawrence	*Wintry Peacock*	Amit Chaudhuri
Rosamond Lehmann	*The Gipsy's Baby*	Niall Griffiths
Carlo Levi	*Words are Stones*	Anita Desai
André Malraux	*The Way of the Kings*	Rachel Seiffert
Katherine Mansfield	*In a German Pension*	Linda Grant
Katherine Mansfield	*Prelude*	William Boyd
Vladimir Mayakovsky	*My Discovery of America*	Colum McCann
Luigi Pirandello	*Loveless Love*	
Françoise Sagan	*The Unmade Bed*	
Jean-Paul Sartre	*The Wall*	Justin Cartwright
Bernard Shaw	*The Adventures of the Black Girl in Her Search for God*	Colm Tóibín
Georges Simenon	*Three Crimes*	
Leonard Woolf	*A Tale Told by Moonlight*	Victoria Glendinning
Virginia Woolf	*Memoirs of a Novelist*	